Down the Chimney They Came

A Holiday Season Novel

Thomas P. Hanna

Down the Chimney They Came

Copyright © 2020 by Thomas P. Hanna

Cover image credits:

Wreath: Freeimages.com/ Rachel Kirk

Cat: Freeimages.com/ Michael and Christi Richert

Goose: Freeimages.com/ Bryan Hardy

Boxes: Freeimages.com/ xxlawrence

Table of Contents

Chapter 01

When Louise Jansen asked her sixteen year old son Toby for a few minutes to explain some things to him, he prepared himself to do what he could to reassure her about whatever was the problem this time. Her expression and hesitation starting as they settled to talk in the living room where they would be most likely to see him if dad got back from his doctor's appointment told him this was not likely about anything he had done.

"I need to warn you about your Aunt Sally," she said.

"I've learned on my own not to trust her," he said.

"That's sort of it. I want to warn you about being too much of a perfectionist. She tends that way and I think that's what drives her to do some of what she does. More exactly, how she does what she does."

"She wants us all to think she have lots of money but I doubt she does," he said.

"Her personal financial reality is that she inherited some money but that was not that much - and that's long gone. You might as well know this. About the time you were born she split a half-million dollar State lottery payout with two other women. She tried to cheat them by saying their shared ticket did not have the exact numbers. But both had phone pics of it that she didn't know about. Also she claimed it in disguise since our State lets the winners stay unidentified if they wish.

'The other two followed her home from a bank where she got cash to cut paper trails to the money. From what I heard, they walked in on her contemplating so much cash. Each took forty percent rather than the one third, since there wouldn't be those paper trails. They dared her to go to police so the whole story would be tabloid fodder."

"What a story that would have made. Wow!"

"For several years after that she worked at hinting that she had *won big* without saying where or how much and many assumed she must be the unnamed lottery winner but she wouldn't say and there was no legal way to find out. The other two were content with that since it kept beggars from their doors as one was quoted as saying."

"Thank you warning me about her. I promise I won't repeat that story except to beat her off. But I'll be thinking about what she might be plotting any time I have to deal with her in any way. What else?"

Toby nodded to indicate he understood where she might want this to go and to encourage her to say what he suspected she had been rehearsing in her head for days.

"Simply put, she's a user and for your own sake you should have as little to do with Sally Dragenlyte as possible." There, she had said it. There was no deciding to not say more now.

Again he said nothing, but nodded to encourage her to say what she thought he ought to hear from her as his protector.

"Your aunt is very ambitious so she tends to take on more that she should and formulates precise perfect schedules and plans. She ends up frantic and furious when some piece of the elaborate plan doesn't go as she envisioned. Then she has to find someone to blame. She doesn't learn from these events and sets herself up for that kind of thing again and again." Okay, basic message delivered.

"Am I a piece of her current plan or the one being blamed for it not working?" he asked.

Lousie was a bit startled that he grasped her line of thought and got right to the point - and relieved that he did so which would make the next part easier.

"Your father getting sick as he has changed our situation. That has created new pressures and time limits on me."

He nodded. "I'm ready to do what I can to help since I know things are shaky. Tell me what we need to do together to get through this scary period."

Again she was surprised and also relieved. He was making this easier but the hardest part was still to be mentioned.

She went on, "Sally works hard at being noticed and knowing when her doing somebody of social or business consequence will rack up favor IOUs. From what I see and hear, she has no great business skill in any specialty but looks nice and willing attends events on the arm of midlevel managers and the sons of the rich who may find the photos of them together awkward later. Her silence or a good word in the right ear can be assured if she gets the favor she asks today."

"What favor is she offering to do for you?" Toby asked calmly.

She almost gasped out loud at his grasp of the situation.

"There's a job that I'm qualified for and have interviewed for. That's where she saw me and connected the dots. Someone there is taking a long time to choose a candidate. She phoned last night. Said she could get someone there to move things along with my name at the top of the list if I arrange help for her on a special project."

"That's where I come into this. Okay, she wants to hire me for some job she can't or doesn't want to be seen doing. Tell me what I'd have to do," Toby said.

Louise noted the *what I'd have to do* rather than *what I have to do* - and relaxed a notch. He might volunteer, but her clever for his age son hadn't promised not to say no.

"I don't know the details but I have an email address to ask for them. I didn't want to seem desperate. That'd be a bad signal to send to someone like her. I have to say right off that I don't expect more than the minimum detail from her."

"Which will reinforce our suspicions that it's something she doesn't want her name associated with and therefore if I make sure I can do that, I have something over her as our protection," he said.

"But if it's clearly illegal or even highly suspicious we'll have nothing to do with it."

"I absolutely agree. I'll be thinking about that a lot. See what she'll tell you in an email that we all know these days lasts forever."

* * *

The email arrived quickly.

"She had this ready and waiting," Louise said.

"Probably means there's a time deadline for getting this done. That's an extra fact I can use," Toby said.

"One person to transfer small items from one set of packages to another. Working alone in a safe warehouse. No nearby parking for cars or bikes."

Toby typed in, "Okay so far, what other stipulations?"

"I'm worried about why she specifies a safe warehouse."

"She expecting me to do it. That's to reassure you," he said.

A new message read: "Must be done between 9 and 11:30 PM this date."

He typed, "Acceptable. Location? Any locked gates or doors?"

The reply was, "Bixby warehouse. Fifteenth and Finchflutter Streets. Open gate by attached garage. Repeat, no nearby parking."

Before his mother could stop him, Tody clicked on the *Accept* button on the screen, then disconnected.

"Wait. Shouldn't you have made demands," Louise asked.

"Those wouldn't go anywhere in court but I have enough time to get ready to avoid anything that can harm us there. And her emails now on our machine can help the police connect her to anything illegal that's involved with whatever I'll be repacking. So many bits fall into place because of her email responses."

"What are you thinking, Toby?"

"That's she needs this done by a definite time suggests that the repackaged goods, whatever they are, must be ready for pickup at midnight."

"I see how that seems likely."

"The *no nearby parking* is to force whoever does it to walk there and be caught on security cameras around a whole warehouse area like that these days. That's to make it be me, not you who goes."

"That seems clever but it means evidence that someone did go into the warehouse," she said.

"But nobody will care about that unless the authorities come looking to find out what happened there because the stuff was illegal."

"I guess you're right. People must walk around there at night just passing by."

"If it's only hand work that shouldn't take more than an hour or two. That she won't do it herself even alone suggests that she's not certain that the items aren't stolen or illegal in some other way and won't risk being involved if they are," he said.

"It make sense when you lay it out."

"She might be tempted to compromise me to keep things over your head to use you again. The simplest way would be to have my fingerprints on things inside the warehouse, and especially on the reboxed things. So from the moment I step onto that place I'll wear food servers gloves and not leave any prints."

"Are your prints on file so they could name you?"

"Not that I know of. Which is what she doesn't know but may think you'll assume must automatically be the case. So the Dragon Lady wants something done, she says do it or she'll anonymously tip the cops to check your son's prints to find out what's he's been involved in. Yeah, I've heard you and dad and the Gordons call her that for years."

"I'm shocked at that thought - but have to admit I have no trouble imagining her doing it to get what she wants."

"But when and if she says that, you remind her that I'll tip the cops to investigate what role she had to do with whatever takes place down there tonight. They don't have to find anything they can charge her with, same as with her tip, they only need to start poking around to light up the whisper world and make her a center of focus in a way she many not survive."

"I feel like maybe I should beg you not to mess with her, but I'm not doing so because I sense that you'll tell me no and ignore me on it."

"Do you honestly believe that there's anything you or I can do that will keep her from trying to punish me for even hesitating to do what she wants? No, don't answer that. Let me tell you that I don't believe so and therefore I have to take charge of protecting myself from her," he said. "And if your new job doesn't work out, she'll regret it."

* * *

At eight-twenty that evening Toby, wearing a plain, dark hoodie over a billed cap and a scarf around his lower face that together largely hid his face from any overhear security cameras, nonchalantly walked the full block around the Bixby Warehouse.

From the moment he arrived, he held his smartphone in one bare hand so it was obvious to anyone who saw him.

At eight-thirty Sally Dragenlyte drove up in a dark sports car and parked across the street and toward the farther intersection. She was also dressed to not be identifiable.

She got out, smiling and humming quietly to herself.

She had planned from early on that if she set up the Jansen brat to do this job she would go inside before he arrived, help herself to a few items - she knew they were pieces of pricey jewelry - and be gone when he arrived. When at midnight the count of items was checked and found to be off, the only person who would be assumed to have had a chance to keep them would be him.

But there was someone who could be either gender and of any age in that outfit standing by the only gate *accidentally* left open so they could get in.

Oh wait, that person raised a hand - and there was a flash of light. Her phone picture had been taken. From a height that would have the greatest chance of enough of her face being seen to identify her.

Then the figure stood still but with the lighted phone panel still visible from down the street. Was that the Jansen kid? Could she storm over there and demand that he delete that picture?

Was him standing there so openly a warning that others were watching her or them both and recording everything? Who might those be? There were too many possibilities and nothing she could see to do that didn't increase the chances of her being documented here.

She got back in the car and drove away.

She noted that the person by the gate didn't move. Should she drive around the block, then slowly pass that person for a better look? No, that could result in a better photo of her. Unhappy, she drove away.

At five after nine, Toby put his phone away and put on vinyl gloves from his pocket, then went through the gate and to the nearest door into the warehouse. He didn't care so he didn't look to see if there was a mechanism that had only let that door open after nine. He also didn't know or care if there was anyone else in there with him.

Where he needed to work was obvious since there was an over-head light on there. The job was also obvious based on the few words he had been told.

A wooden crate with the top pried off sat on a work table. Inside were about fifty smallish items, each in a sealed plastic bag with only a few ID numbers on it. On the other side of the table was a open carton. Beside it were stacks of small empty gift boxes used by a nationally known jewelry company. His job was to open each bag, put its contents in a small box, then put that in the carton. Nothing more than that.

He didn't know or need to know the why, he got right to work on the transferring. He barely glanced at the jewelry pieces since he had no interest.

He was relieved but tried not to show that or any emotion that there were the same number of bags and boxes; no left-overs or empty boxes that might be problems.

And he never touched anything coming in, doing the job, and now leaving without gloves on his hands. He suspected there were cameras on him the whole time but he never looked to spot them. As long as he did every move as openly as possible, he felt safe. Whatever videos were made would clearly show he was gloved. He wondered if those who made those would tell Aunt Sally that.

He found an envelope marked *For Your Trouble* with cash in it taped to the inside of the door to outside. He pocketed that and left. He hadn't been expecting that, but felt sure it was intended for him. By whom was another bit he didn't need to know. He doubted that Aunt Sally left that there and wondered if she would ever know about it. Not from him anyway, since cash was not part of his deal with her.

Outside he closed the gate behind him - securing it closed was not his job - and walked away.

Two blocks away he could get a city bus home. He didn't bother to try to spot anyone watching him as he went.

He got the bus and went home. He would hear on the morning news, soon enough for his purposes, if the Bixby Warehouse was raided by any authority after he was gone. He didn't care since he had picked up no clear signals that anything was illegal, only that some of the people involved were not entirely sure they could trust the others.

*   *   *

Dragenlyte had acted as an anonymous agent - with all contacts by phone - to arrange the job. She also got some cash but no contacts she could use again later without possible problems for revealing too much. But cash was necessary. When payment to the worker had been mentioned she insisted such money be given to her to deliver. The idea was not mentioned to her again so she assumed it had not been done.

That annoyed her since she could use that extra sum - and she had not even tempted the boy with it so she would not be reneging on the promise of a fraction of what she was given.

Ms. Dragenlyte was amazed at how fast she could go through what to many was a substantial amount of money when intent on being seen as living the lifestyle she couldn't really afford but was determined to have by hook or by crook. Literally if necessary, as she had shown.

Whether or not it had been Toby Jansen standing outside and effectively scaring her off from helping herself to a few pieces of good quality jewelry to sell as she had intended. she would blame him for it. For that and a list of other offenses, great and small - she was big on making lists for her own eyes only - she would hassle that boy to get some satisfaction from her not glorious enough life. He deserved it.

Chapter 02

That Ms. Sally Dragenlyte was not happy at the moment would not be news to many who had dealings with her. In fact many of them would describe it as the usual situation - even to her face. That reality is what brought her here to plot a new life strategy today.

She was in the room at the back of the Dornic family's garage while she was certain they were away today. They didn't know her and would have been surprised to find her there. If she ever had to, and she would avoid that if at all possible, she would argue that by leaving a key to the garage doors poorly hidden outside they had invited anyone willing to take the time to search a bit inside to use the space.

She never checked whether the other hidden key was to the house or even went close to it. She neither took anything from the garage nor hid anything in there.

It was simply a place to work at her laptop with minimum worry that her files were being or could be monitored by others when she was riled up. There was more than a mere tinge of paranoia to her concerns since she had been using information she got by snooping on their personal files to help herself or mess with others for years now. Most people wouldn't care what she said about them since the feelings were likely mutual, but those she still hoped to influence or to use in some way might be put off.

She had her machine checked for leaks often - and by a different independent tech each time since she didn't trust any company doing that kind of work not to regularly at least be offered bribes for access.

Wearing a disguise, paying a generous amount of cash, but not volunteering ID, she would describe what she wanted checked for, then sat and waited as that was done, her laptop never out of her sight.

Her personal history was what brought her here today to thrash out some changes. She wasn't getting any younger and she was hardly any better situated beyond the short-term than when she started out on her own.

For the better part of two decades on her own she tried to *be nice* her way up the social ladder. She got enough money to maintain the illusion that she had plenty, but not from any company payroll that would have required her to have a formal contract. She accepted playing unofficial-helper as the price to meet people whom she hoped would open more doors for her. She became moderately widely known in local high society, but not especially respected or liked.

Then recently she was dumped with no warning or remorse when someone with better computer and people skills came along and soon became the official, with a formal contract, assistant.

As she sought solace in what she expected to be a torrent of messages of sympathy online, she came across online addresses where she found substantial collections of easy to guess the source of rumors about negative things she said and did over those years, with hints of details recorded.

Now she trusted no one but herself but would still kiss up at least a bit to new people whom she might be able to use until she knew them and their assets well enough to decide if they were worth the effort and the social liability if they fell out of favor.

By now she had convinced herself that the recent major change in her social status was because she had been too nice. Not nice in most people's definition, but nice in the sense that she had not been meeting the world's indifference or only mild interest in her with hard nastiness until she chose to graciously ease up out of sympathy for those who were fortunate enough to get to deal with her.

She actually typed that into her machine, reread it with a wide satisfied smile, and ceremoniously tapped the keys to save it.

She sat for a long moment trying slight variations on that smile. Facial expressions and body language could be useful tools. As another part of her security concerns, she routinely disconnected her laptop's webcam when she was not making contacts so she could not avoid being recorded by the contact person later or those snooping in.

At these off-system times, she put a mirror on a stand beside the machine to study herself as she pondered different topics and the messages her face was sending in addition to her words.

"Mirror, Mirror, not on a wall, I don't care about your estimate about my fairness of the face skin-deep type, I need you to help me train myself to get over any lingering old-fashioned restraints about fairness in the harsh spheres of reality holding me back from full success. I need to snarl silently and stare holes in people to scare them into doing whatever I say. Or, if I can marry money and he's at least as presentable as Austin Noble, that'll be an acceptable alternative to more direct conquest."

She took another full minute to practice smiles with underlying messages but could not convince herself that those would be readable to anyone not hearing the desired interpretation shouted at them.

"Yes, Sally, I hear the voice that won't shut up reminding me that there's not much money left under the mattress and big questions about who's gonna give me more without expecting me to have more skills than I do. I'm an experienced people charmer-then-cheater but my head doesn't get computers," she told herself.

She practiced expressions to elicit sympathy without pity.

"I can't help it if computers confuse me. I can follow a list of printed steps to make some program work but I get lost and irritated when I know others know there are ways to make the machine do some stuff faster or with fewer steps but I can't read the instructions on those parts and make any sense of them. And nobody's rushing to tutor me about them. Even those I offer to pay to teach me - but only when I describe myself as being proficient - won't let me use and cheat them."

She gestured into the mirror that she was finally facing facts.

"Okay, I'll say it you, Mirror, but it goes no farther. Understood? Yeah, things that I've done when I moved faster than the others were smart enough for my purposes to do did damage me in some circles."

She wagged a warning finger at the mirror.

"We agreed a while back - how long is no more important than the rest - never to use *mis-* words for what I've done, only for what others did. I'm not going to change that. Probably ever."

She glanced around, confirming for herself that she was alone.

"The important point for me to remember is that I was admired for doing those things I won't put that word on. So my emphasis on firmness isn't entirely new, I'll just emphasize it more. I've pretended not to hear the 'dragon lady' comments all this time, now I'll embrace that name. But I'll never call myself it. Or let anybody - anybody - call me that to my face. Well, without objecting. Okay, I guess that's a contradiction but just one more in a list of them. *Grrr!*"

She examined the laptop monitor for hints of her reflection but with it booted up all she was the text of her current notes.

"I'll actively look for chances to practice being mean even if I then decide at times not to do that openly. When I think about it, cases where you have to analyze what was done to realize it was deliberate meanness are even more impressive. Hey, maybe I should review the detailed notes I keep on this machine about my recent past actions to maybe make sure those I targeted know - without solid proof, of course - that I was behind what happened."

She smiled at that thought, then wiped that expression.

"Or maybe not. How much is too much is tricky since it can be different depending on who gets snarled at and who's seen by a whole audience as snarling in a petty situation."

She looked at her reflection and shook her head sadly.

"I've been at this too long to not be more successful. Who can I blame for that? There has to be someone. At least naming them to myself would make me feel better. As this point any bit better helps. How can I explain it all away to others I still want to impress? Between you and me, mirror, I'm thinking more and more that's what to try?"

Then she got angry.

"I never did anything really bad to the Jansens or the Gordons so why wouldn't they lavish praise on me when people asked about me before giving me access to their belongings and contacts? I didn't ask them if it would be okay, I just listed them as references expecting them to feel honored to be asked to give me star ratings since I'm a relative. I could have profited from at least some of those contacts. They never mentioned being asked - but we have almost no contacts or reasons to have them. From what some of those who said 'thanks anyway' to me said those relatives didn't make open accusations about me, only said they wouldn't recommend me. That hurt. They're on my get revenge list. When a chance comes along, *bang,* they get hurt."

She reacted with fear and surprise to her image in the mirror.

"Wow! Good thing I saw that even if it scared me. Can't let the revenge face show unless I intend to punish-scare somebody I'm sure I'll have no more use for."

She shuddered as she made sure that look was gone.

"I have to go across the State line and work in backrooms with no contact with the public but I can keep some cash coming in cleaning up the English in the paperwork that a few foreign companies send Americans. Most have their own in-house people and many of them don't do a good job but I can't let anybody else know what I'm doing."

As she shuts down the laptop and put the mirror in her tote bag she looked around to be sure she would take away everything she brought in.

She said, "I never quite intended people to wonder where my money comes from but that's a more likely question than ever today and what I fear being asked more than ever before when I'm trying to keep up this glamorous false front. Life's not fair. But then again neither am I or I maybe wouldn't be in this situation."

Chapter 03

The year that Toby Jansen was born, Sally Dragenlyte turned thirty (but of course didn't admit to that many years). After too many years of straining to pretend she was better off than she was, this was a good one for Sally's wallet.

The complication she had to accept for that financial windfall - that she truly did have to work hard for - was that she could not brag about it or even mention it. It wouldn't help if those she still wanted and needed to impress connected her to the last time certain items were seen by the public - or their whereabouts confirmed - after a questionable transaction she pulled off.

After a decade of subtly dropping hints that she might be open to sneaky or even strong arm tactics to get what a patron willing to pay for her help wanted, in 2001 she was picked up on a downtown street by a taxi at a pre-arranged time and spot.

In the back seat, she found herself alone but with a cell phone waiting in a box along with a sealed envelope as the driver seemed to ignore her and drove them around downtown.

"I'm ready, so tell me what you want so I can decide if I'm able and willing to help you," she said into that phone.

"I'm a collector. I want to add two large items from the town of Festivity. Are you familiar with the town?" a man asked from it.

"No, but if it's on maps I should have no trouble finding it if I have an interest in doing so. What are the items?" she asked.

"Large props from an old silent movie donated in 1922 by the director to someone he wanted to impress who promptly donated them to that town where they've been a minor tourist attraction ever since," the Collector said.

"Are they in some kind of a museum?"

"They are a major part of the town's only two in-town traffic lights. They stand a block apart."

"You want their old traffic lights?" Dragenlyte asked.

"Not quite. Each of them is a tall hollow wooden tube that opens up on one side. With a fancy wood star on top. When the town needed traffic lights they fitted the tubes around those and fixed it so the lights show on both side but the wires and everything to control them is inside or collected through small holes through the tubes. My sources tell me they could be quickly and easily removed without damaging or removing the traffic light poles," the Collector said.

"Do I have this right? You want someone to go and steal the fancy covers from around this town's only two traffic lights?"

"Not *steal* them, *buy* them. Since they haven't announced them for sale the person secretly acting as my agent has to find who can legally sell them and persuade him, her, or them to do so."

"That sounds like a challenge and a half. Why would they sell off their tourist attraction?" she asked.

"Open the envelope. The amount on the small paper is what I'm ready to put where you can easily get it in cash."

Dragenlyte stared shocked but very excited at the number on the page from the envelope. "That much? Wow, I see why they should be glad to sell you some old wooden tubes."

"I want what I want and I'm willing to pay for it. I can't send you there to just feel them out about selling, my first proxy contact has to take them by pleasant surprise and close a deal fast before things bog down with outsiders involved and some too eager to know who I am."

"Is it safe for me to be talking to you while I'm in this cab?"

"He's okay. And he can't hear a word if asked by officials at some future time," the Collector said.

"That tells me a lot."

"I hoped so. The less I have to spell out, the better for us both."

"Okay. Do you require a written sales receipt?"

"With the several marked spaces filled in, the standard pages in the envelope should serve the purpose and speed the process by not requiring the seller to get a form prepared. Copy for him, copy for us."

Dragenlyte scanned the large pages.

"No mention of your name or a company name."

"But a designation that should suffice for legal purposes since that shouldn't happen for some time after the cash money and items of interest have changed hands and disappeared into the night."

"Hint, hint?" Dragenlyte asked.

"A gentle one. If you agree to try to do this of course I'll monitor you, but I won't contact you or let you contact me. And I won't fuss about what name you sign on the papers as long as there's little chance you'll be questioned before you and the prizes are away from the town."

"How am I supposed to get those big things away from there?"

"You'd be in charge and should use some of the money to hire help to get them into a truck. It'd be foolish and self-defeating to try to do that yourself. I can give you names of people I'd trust to help, get paid, and forget they were ever involved. You or they drive the truck to a designated spot where my man will confirm what are in the truck and take charge of my new pleasures."

"All neatly worked out. Why bother to involve me in it?"

"It needs an artful liar to get it done fast before more than a few locals know anything is astir, much less what it is," the Collector said.

"Is that supposed to be flattery?" she asked with a smile.

"I expect you to think so. One last point before you give me an answer. I transfer the sum on the note to where you can get it in cash with no paper trail. You pay all your expenses out of that. All of them. Whatever's left is yours."

That widened her smile.

He went on, "That may prod you to be as cheap as possible at several points but let me be clear that if you fail at this I will get back every dollar except what I alone, decide were reasonable expenses. And note that I didn't say I'll *try* to get the money back, I will."

"Goodness. That tone gives me second and third thoughts about this," she said.

"Say 'No thanks' and all of this was just a daydream. But say yes and it'll have the weight of a contract between us."

She took a deep breath, but then let that out and said, "I agree to try on your terms."

"The driver has another envelope for you. Everything else you need. Where to get the cash. Photos of the items of interest. Safe people to hire as helpers with a truck. Beyond that you're on your own."

"Will I ever see you to talk about this?"

"You'd better hope not."

*　*　*

Three days later Ms. Dragenlyte drove herself to the Town of Festivity, arriving a bit after ten A.M., and found the small town center just as the photos in the second envelope showed it.

She wore a ton of makeup to look older and clothes she thought looked *small town no fashion* sense for her purposes of being forgettable.

She ignored the *No Parking* sign and walked over to examine the nearer of the two tubes that housed the traffic lights.

She took digital camera pics of it, then tapped on the wood tube.

With no locks in sight to stop her, she removed the twisted wires keeping one tube closed to see how things were attached inside.

At that point twentyish local handyman John Febbraro came over to check on her doing.

"Who are you and why did you open that?" he asked as he moved between her and the open tube, letting his muscular bulk force her back a step. "What did you do with the wires?"

"They had fallen off and were on the ground," she lied as she pointed to where she had tossed them aside.

"No they weren't. Keep your hands off what doesn't belong to you," he said firmly as he reclosed the tube with the wires.

"I can do whatever I please," she said defiantly.

So fast she gasped, she found his fist firm against her face. "Then we'll feel sure you wanted your face pounded to make it less ugly. Keep your hands off things."

He turned and walked away, not looking back.

She had casually lied to test how that strategy would work here. Maybe not well. At least she had to avoid this guy if possible. She didn't know his name. She thought about taking his pic with her phone but decided his angry look and the strangeness of her asking strangers to identify one of their own from a photo she took of him was a bad idea.

Trying to seem unmoved about her first encounter with a town members, Dragenlyte walked the block between the traffic lights and a block beyond that on either end, up one side of the street and down the other, assessing the buildings and the condition of everything in view.

She was not impressed, but had arrived determined not to be. These must be simple bumpkins or her plan to buy the silly tubes dirt cheap would not work and she refused to think it might not happen.

Already she was shifting from a plan to buying the tubes from the town officials with talk about how much good that money could do the town that was no tourist draw anyway. She was determined to convince herself this could be done with the fewest problems by not even applying officially to buy the tubes.

One storefront office was the town's Historical Society. A sign in the window listed a phone number to call if you needed help but said they did not have anyone here on scheduled hours.

Several large and well done posters in the window did a nice job of capsulizing the town's basic history.

Her adjusted strategy required her to show her social skills and get introduced to the town's important people without quite calling them that. She intended to present herself as only curious, not with any interest in business or official matters.

But the only person she had seen here so far was the man who had threatened her nose in response to her mouth lying to him. John Febbraro was making repairs to the outside of a shop - and watching what she was doing.

She told herself she loved a challenge - and sneered but hid that. She ambled up to Febbraro trying to seem casual and that what was done was forgotten. "Perhaps you can help me..."

"Not a chance," he said, without stopping what he was doing or looking at her. His body language shouted that that would not change.

Then Mrs. Lipinski came out of a nearby shop and Dragenlyte ran to her, new plan started. "Hello. I'm new here and not getting a helpful reception. I'm the noted historian Betsy Brightly. You may have heard of me. I'm busy putting together the complete history of this State. Can you be gracious and tell me the names of those in charge of the town and its physical properties. The list I have is out of date."

Mrs. Lipinski always wanted to be helpful but she was in a hurry right now. Also she sensed that this was an appeal to lead this woman around and she especially didn't have time to do that.

"I have a pie in the oven so I can't take the time to try to explain our loose situation right now. Maybe tomorrow. Are you staying out at the Passing-Bye Motel?"

"I was hoping to pay for lodging with a family here in town to be close and *feel the place*. Maybe with older people who know some of the town's history," Dragenlyte said. She smiled because only she knew how she had considered saying *old people like you* to watch the reaction.

At that moment Fred Quade came around the corner and looked up and down the street to check that things seemed to be in order.

"That's Fred Quade. Ask him about everything," Mrs. Lipinski said, then hurried away to avoid any further discussion.

As Dragenlyte assessed Quade, a man a few years older than she would admit to being, neatly dressed in standard clothes with little fashion to go out of, and an air of organization about him. Yeah, she could get what she wanted from him.

As she ambled toward Quade, Febbraro strode over to get to Quade first. He made a quiet comment, nodding to indicate her, then stepped back, clearly intending to watch and listen.

Quade now turned and focused on the woman with a different tone of interest than he might otherwise have had. Wary but not openly hostile - so far.

"Hello and welcome to the Town of Festivity," he said blandly.

"I've read a lot about your town and came to see it for myself.".

"I'd love to know what and where you've read about us. We have a young woman who tried to search out references to us on the Internet as a school project and found very little," he said.

"I'm a historian so I know how to do a search," Dragenlyte said.

"Our neighbor was being guided by two history professors at the State university."

"I come to find out what I don't know about the town, not what I already do." There, that should end that line of inquiry from him.

She was annoyed, more than worried, as Quade turned enough to exchange silent facial expression messages with Febbraro. They each noted her reaction but showed no concern about it.

"I hope I don't need more than a minute of your time - either of you. Please tell me who's in charge of the town and its properties."

"How technical an answer do you need?" Quade asked.

"I don't understand the question," she said.

"We have a committee who have to make big decisions about matters like spending town money or selling off town property. We have an informal mayor who has a general nod of pre-approval to decide alone about small stuff. What do you need a decision about?" Quade asked. Febbraro silently nodded agreement off to the side.

"Who's this *informal* mayor?"

"For some years now, that's me," Quade said. "You didn't find anything about that arrangment in what you've read about us?"

"Obviously not everything that's written down makes sense. But that makes it even more important for me to talk to a few who know about those unusual details in the town's history," she said.

She hesitated to decide which way to try this, then said, "Is there a diner or restaurant where I can treat some of you to dinner and the management won't throw us out if we get wound up and go late?"

"How about this? You get a motel room outside town and have your dinner, then come to my house for dessert. Once a week we invite a few neighbors to join us. They might know what you want to learn."

"Better still, I'd be happy to pay you to let me stay with you for the night to cut down on the driving around," she said.

"I would never surprise me wife with an unexpected overnight guest and she's away and won't be back until then, bringing dinner for the two of us with her. So that won't work."

"But surely…"

"Or we can forget the whole thing," he said firmly.

Febbraro nodded and silently but openly applauded him.

She forced a smile and held out a piece of paper and a pencil for him to write down the address. She'd make him pay for this later.

Quade wrote that down, then handed them back to her saying, "Seven-thirty. Don't be early. I'll need time to get them primed for what you're interested in so we don't waste a lot of time on tangents."

"I'm sure that would be fine," she said.

"From what I've seen of you only this far, I can only imagine you climbing the walls. And the rest of us crying from boredom because we've heard the stories too many time before. No, seven-thirty. Before that we'll keep you waiting on the porch."

"Come on, now we're bring silly…"

Quade kept a blank face as he raised a cautionary finger.

Febbraro smiling in anticipation of watching her be disinvited was too much. She had to demonstrate how to deal with yokels.

"As almost anyone can see, sir, it makes little sense for you to make things harder than necessary for someone like me trying to put you on real world maps."

Quade politely saluted her, then walked away as he said, "The motel people get paid for ignoring noise. Make them earn their few dollars. Watch out for the dog. He can be mean around fakes."

* * *

Seldom one to not have a back up ready if first plan didn't work out as she planned, Dragenlyte went to and drove away in her car.

She stopped by a pay phone in a gas station at the edge of town and called the phone number on the sign in the town's Historic Society office window. Elderly Miss Clara Doorwatche answered, surprised but happy to have someone call on that number.

In not as short order as she would have liked, Dragenlyte had scheduled Miss Doorwatche to meet her at the office at ten A.M. tomorrow and sit there to let her go through files. She was subtle but the older woman happily understood that it would be worth her while to cooperate.

Chapter 04

Dessert night rotated among a group of long-term townies so the small gathering in the Quade's dining room had been scheduled two weeks before. It was routine courtesy to let the hosts know a week in advance if you expected to attend. There were three likelies and two in-and-outs on the list tonight, plus the hosts Fred and Ramona.

Mrs. Lipinski and her adult son Billy stopped in to say hello to everyone, then left to attend to family matters.

John Febbraro was on the list but cancelled after lunch saying he feared the nosy lady would show up even disinvited and cause a fuss and he might hurt her and not really be sorry for doing it. Better not to take a chance.

Dennis Handerham was there with photos of his pet billy goat named Sergeant and fifteen minutes of stories about what Sergeant had gotten into but wasn't supposed to since the last of these dessert gatherings he had attended.

The others smiled, listened, laughed, and enjoyed their choice of pie, cake, and/or ice cream.

Lucius Knuckles was a regular at these events but seldom had anything interesting to share about his recent activities. He had been born in town, moved away after high school, and only returned when his parents died and he inherited the house where he grew up.

If anyone knew what he did for a living or to pass the time, they didn't share that information. That left a hole to be filled with rumors and suspicions but few seemed interested enough to fill it in from him or any other sources. Two definite knowns were that he put the house on the market even before he arrived, eager to get away from his memories of Festivity. And that he drank heavily and didn't always make it home before he passed out. Tonight he was quiet but polite - and had obviously started his evening of drinking before he arrived.

Rudolf Rambler came to the dessert evenings whenever he could make them for free dessert and to talk about his Christmas gifts to himself since most who met him found him a pleasant diversion. He would describe in unself-conscious detail his reactions to his bought-for-himself experiences to share them, not to make his audience of the moment jealous. He simply had a gift of great gab.

This time he started by reliving his decision and buying search for a jigsaw with which he planned to and did make decorations for his house. He told about why he chose the designs for some of the items he made and gave away rather than on those he kept.

He quietly told how one old woman heard of his gifts to himself and thought he gave himself a jigsaw puzzle. She offered him a stack of them she had in a closet. He made her six coasters that fitted together puzzle-style to a flower shape saying she inspired him.

* * *

While they enjoyed his story inside, Dragenlyte sneaked around outside the house - can of pepper spray ready if there was a dog.

She tested the back kitchen door and since it was unlocked, she crept inside. She was quite proud of herself.

* * *

Next, Rambler described, with emphasis on his thinking as he decided what to give himself, how he had studied up, thought about it for two full weeks - then bought himself sky diving lessons.

This was an exception to his usual routine because he did not insist take the first lesson on Christmas Eve. He avoided the question of whether he would have gone up by noting that both the instructor and pilot said no to that timing. Especially after dark.

He didn't hesitate for dramatic effects since he was pretty sure all except Lucius knew the rest. He admitted that by January second, the first date he could have had a lesson, he had decided not to take them after all. But he didn't ask for any money back since would mean he didn't give himself a present that Christmas Eve.

* * *

Not sure what she might find but with an idea of what she would like to, Dragenlyte eased open the under countertop drawers, then closed them again. She didn't bother with any of the cabinets. If she was going to find it, it would be in a safe-from-splatters drawer where it would also be out of sight.

The kitchen table had a drawer. And what she hoped for, even though it was a long shot.

She had to move fast. That's what a smartphone was for. With the door to the next room closed a photoflash would not be a problem.

She closed the drawer, pondered a moment - then went and stepped back outside but stayed near the closed door with an overhead light that she flipped on as she went out. Now a bit of banking. She had made transactions like this before and months ago had set things up that she could use now although she didn't plan this case back then.

* * *

Rambler's last rambling of the evening was a quick reliving of the fun the year he gave himself a propane grille and cooked Christmas dinner in his yard in a snowstorm. It had been the storm of a decade and he was getting into descriptions he remembered from news reports when he stopped when the doorbell rang.

The Quades exchanged worried looks and started to get up.

Dragenlyte wasn't going to wait to be invited in this time. She sashayed in, looking the house over like a department store window display she didn't really approve of but those without her fine tastes might be okay with.

She announced, "I knew you'd have come to your senses by now and I'm willing to forgive and forget your dumb mistake."

Without a word, Rambler and Handerhan hurried out. Knuckles settled back to see how this would go.

Dragenlyte smirked at the two men who turned sideways to pass her without making contact. Then she noticed Knuckles and was happy to have an audience as well as targets.

"Who are you?" Ramona Quade demanded.

"Didn't - I assume that's your husba…"

"That's not a name. Have you forgotten whatever fake one you used earlier along with your manners and whatever whiff of sense you ever had, if you ever had any?" Ramona asked.

Dragenlyte was taken aback for a moment, then opted to go with a dismissal strategy. She stepped closer so she could face Fred and be partly turned from Ramona. "You should keep your little woman…"

She stopped and took two steps back as Ramona stood and faced her - holding up the large knife there to cut desserts.

"Your name or your fat butt on its way fast back out that door," Ramona growled and stepped toward her.

Dragenlyte backed as she rethought her strategy since Fred was looking at the pie on the table, not at his wife and the threat she was directing at the pushy broad who had chosen to burst in on them.

"As I told the men this morning, I'm historian Betsy Brightly. I came to this town at the request of a major publisher to check if it's interesting enough to write about."

"What publisher?" Ramona asked, moving the knife blade side to side as if eager to use it.

She had memorized the Brightly name and historian bits on her way here this morning. The publisher was a nice touch she added just now under pressure. Good going, Sally!

"We don't have a finished contract yet so I'm not at liberty to mention the name."

Ramona said, "You can't think of one with a credible name to lie about? You're clearly not good at anything you try to do. That certainly applies…" She chuckled with disdain, "Applies like you trowel on cheap makeup to hide under. Or maybe you have a spark of decency and want the spare us the hideous reality." Then she sat back at the table.

Dragenlyte stared into space for a long moment, reconsidering her plan. She had set things up but then these people didn't react as she expected and needed them to. What would have been straight-forward unapologetic pressure suddenly could be messy, messy, messy.

Trying for wounded pride as she relaxed a bit at not having wounded flesh so far, Dragenlyte said, "We got off on a bad foot but I'm dedicated to my project. You don't have a sampling of the town folks here for me to debrief but I'll stand by our deal to pay you to put me up for the night here while you call in the neighbors to facinate me."

"You proposed and I said no. That means there never was any deal except to go our separate ways," Fred Quade said.

"That means you get out now," Ramona said.

"If you insist but it will be awkward for you. Maybe tie up your bank accounts for weeks if I must file a complaint about being cheated. Probably make the news as the new way for old towns to stay relevant."

Ramona was focused on the bits of cut lawn grass on the floor from the front door to Dragenlyte's shoes. Then she looked around as if seeing someone walking around the house on the lawn that had been mowed that afternoon.

Fred was focused on Dragenlyte's words. "Why could you claim we cheated you for saying no to your offer to intrude on us?"

"On the basis of our deal I transferred two hundred dollars into your bank account as a generous payment for a night's stay," she said.

Ramona went to the kitchen door, opened it and turned on the overhead light, then looked carefully at the floor from there.

She turned back and stared with disbelief at Dragenlyte who smiled politely, confident she had them as she intended.

Fred and Knuckles watched this with no idea what it meant.

As Ramona walked into the kitchen, Fred asked Dragenlyte, "How could you do what you say you did? That doesn't make sense."

Ramona came back out and to the table carrying the Quades bank account book and checkbook.

"She came in the back door at some point, found our bank books where we keep them to be convenient. She transferred money from her account to ours using online banking. All she needed was our account number to receive it. She knew an approval signal for money to leave her account, but our account didn't need one to approve receiving it," Ramona said.

Dragenlyte smiled and flaunted latex gloves from her handbag.

"She wore gloves so her fingerprints won't be on anything in our kitchen and only the grass clippings she tromped in and out of there and then in our front door show what happened," Ramona said.

"Such a fanciful story. I should recommend you to the publisher but they don't print nonfiction. And the libel laws protect we innocents from malicious lies," Dragenlyte said.

"Get out of here now," Fred ordered.

"With that you make the cheat official. Expect to hear from the Court in short order if I don't get satisfaction," Dragenlyte said.

At that, Ramona hurried into the living room - with Fred close behind her since he suspected what she wanted.

Fred was right and grabbed his wife firmly from behind to keep her in place but made no move to take the fireplace poker from her.

"I want some satisfaction too," Ramona said.

"Since you've chosen to be rude as well as cheats it's only right that you should call for a taxi to take me to the motel - and pay for my night there. You can arrange that by phone with a credit card."

"If I lose my grip here, you'd better be running out the door and all the way to whoever'll have you or I predict a rearrangment of parts of your head," Fred said.

Just then two large and agitated dogs began barking outside. Dragenlyte opened the front door to see what was going on. At that the dogs pulled loose - or were released, who can say for sure - and charged for the porch and the door.

Rambler was out there with the dogs owner but he seemed to be looking at the sky unaware of the action here.

Dragenlyte closed the door, making sure it was tightly shut.

She held her head high and radiated disdain from these little people as she dialed her phone.

The voice was loud so all four people heard, "This is a recording. Everyone on the county police departments is dealing with a major multivehicle crash. Pleae call back in the morning or seek other help."

Dragenlyte fumbled and almost dropped the phone as she tried to dial another number as Ramona Quade made her first real effort to pull free of Fred and use the poker.

Then the unexpected way out of the problem happened. Lucius Knuckles called to Dragenlyte, "My car's out front. I can give you ride somewhere if you want."

Dragenlyte looked at him. When she literally first saw him, she had dismissed him as useless except as a witness if what he saw might help her and she had been ignoring his since. Now he was a solution.

"Thank you, that would be proper and correct. I've had enough of being cheated and threatened for one evening," she said.

"Yeah, yeah. You sure pile it high and still keep at it. No wonder nobody wants to be around you unless they have something to gain before you figure a way to cheat them," Knuckles said as he headed for the front door. "Thanks for the desserts. The cake was the best," he said with a wave to the Quades.

When the door closed behind those two, Fred released Ramona who gave him the poker and headed upstairs. "Where are you going?" he called after her.

"To call Mary Ann's daughter. She's the high school's whiz at searching the internet. I want to see what she can find, or not find, about a historian named Bestsy Brightly. Especially a photo or at least an age. Just to satisfy my liar-detection sense."

* * *

On the ride to the motel, Dragenlyte said, "I might have use for your skills on a job I have to do."

"You mean you'd like to use me and dump me," he said.

"Now don't go off on a snit."

"Lady, I think we can profit from one another, then go off our separate ways not wanting or expecting to ever see one another again. Tell me what you think you can pull off and let's see if I can help out or tell you where the pitfalls will be but maybe suggest how you can avoid those if the price is right. And I only deal in cash."

"Are you a cop?"

He snorted a guffaw and shook his head in disbelief.

"I'm a guy looking for a stake to let me escape from this whole area and never look back. Check me out. Lucius Knuckles. I'm sure you have contacts you can make who'll let you in on my whole boring story."

"Suppose I don't decide to use you."

"Then you'll make things harder for yourself but it won't have changed my situation. Won't make it better, also won't make it worse. I am gonna charge you for this taxi ride though. One of my favorite bars needs to be kept in business at least one more night."

"Okay. This is what I need to do and how I plan to pull it off."

Chapter 05

The next morning "Betsy Brightly" went to some trouble to be sure she was noticed having breakfast at the motel.

She had paid for two nights with a prepaid credit card and a fake ID while Knuckles kept the desk clerk's attention mostly on him as if he wanted to sneak to where he had not paid to go. They had stopped along the way to let her pick up her own car. That whole operation earned him a big cash tip.

She left her car there, and dressed and made up as Ms. Brightly took the local taxi to the Historic Society office arriving at 10 A.M.

There Mrs. Doorwatche proved more helpful than her visitor had dared to hope for. With someone seeming to actually want to hear about such things, the guardian of the old facts revealed that since old Town Hall was badly damaged by fire five years back, many town papers, some maybe the only copies, were stored in locked files here in this office. Of course she has access to keys. Plus, all on the files were on microfiche to make searching fast and easy. There might be originals on paper in the file cases but what was on them was there in that form too. There were still no solid plans to rebuild Town Hall.

* * *

At their bank, Ramona Quade confirmed the transfer of $200 into the Quade account as of 9 A.M. that day.

The Manager admitted things were unusual but not illegal or on the face of it improper. The account supplying the money had been closed down as soon as that transfer was done so there was no way to reverse or undo it because no longer an account to send it back to. And the account owner was identified by a number, not a name, so he couldn't tell Ramona who sent the money.

* * *

Fred Quade entered the Historical Society Office at 1:35 P.M. with John Febbraro along a witness.

Literally a minute before that the phone rang and Mrs. Doorwatche moved to another room where things would be quieter to answer it. The unidentified caller would keep her talking until signaled.

While Febbraro took video of them, Quade handed her a check made out to Betsy Brightly for $200 drawn on his account as her refund. Dragenlyte accepted it.

"How interesting. But this piece of paper doesn't change anything until I deposit it. If it got lost or, maybe accidentally shredded..."

Febrraro leaned down and said quietly but distinctly, "There might be consequences your survivors would describe as unfortunate."

She stumbled to her feet in dramatic indignation. "How dare you threaten me! I should call the police and report this right now."

"Do that. Or I'll do it if you want to pretend to be too shaken up to talk. We want any investigation of you by any law authority, local, State or Federal. They'll all have to start at the same place. Your legal identity. We'll see what all will unwind from there," Febbraro said.

Quade took Febbraro by the shoulder and, muttering calming things, led him out. "You're too close to hitting her, John. That'll cause more trouble than she's worth."

The two men walked out and the call that was occupying Mrs. Doorwatche ended.

Dragenlyte took the taxi back to the motel at 4 P.M. to be seen.

* * *

At midnight, three men, wearing black sweats, ski masks to hide their faces, and gloves, quietly drove a truck to the center of town.

Leaving the motor running, they lowered a ramp from the back edge to the street to make getting inside easy.

Dragenlyte, dressed like them but with her mask hat not rolled down, drove her car up and parked nearby while she came to supervise.

Moving quickly since they knew what to expect, the gloved men clipped the wire closers on the one wood tube, slid it sideways from around the traffic light pole, careful not to snag and drag any wires, then reclosed the tube with masking tape.

In a move virtually rehearsed several times. One man straight-arm pushed it over away from him at chest-height - as the second walked his hands up the side that was coming down on him - as the third prepared to and then did grab the wider top wooded star.

An adjustment of grips, a grunt to coordinate them - and they picked it and carried it up the ramp and into the truck where they had moving van pads stacked to receive it and hold it in place.

Dragenlyte had gone up the ramp ahead of them and made sure that the pads had not moved since she checked them fifteen minutes earlier before she gave the nod to start the operation.

The driver started to get off - then remembered and gestured for the boss of the hour to go first. So she was first to be photographed.

Elaine Wurster smelled a rat. There was no proper reason for the town to let anyone load the old movie prop into an unmarked truck in the middle of the night without telling everyone first.

At this time Wurster was a year out of high school, a bit below average on the height scale, had a head full of permed curls, a twitch in her left eye, and a determination to protect the world from liars and cheats. But not as an official, especially not a police officer, with her tendency to get angry and say and do what would let too many perps walk free because of her passion.

Wurster took thirty seconds of video, then she charged over to challenge Dragenlyte who stood nodding at how well this was going.

"Whoever you are, I'll bet you have no permission from the town to even touch that thing," Wurster said.

"You're nobody so nobody cares what you'll bet on," Dragenlyte said. Then she whispered to herself, "But you do have a video camera. That's a problem I need to deal with."

Dragenlyte tested the situation. She took two steps toward Wurster. Wurster took one step backwards to keep at a distance but okay being closer. Especially as she looked things over and planned the views she could video record of the truck and the item now inside it that shouldn't be.

The truck driver came down the ramp, turned and raised that, with the other two men still unseen by the new woman inside.

Dragenlyte was alarmed that he had acted without a signal from her - and was now ignoring her. He got in the cab and drove away. He judged the situation and, experienced at thefts in the night, decided it was best to act like they knew they were allowed to do this.

Wurster was more confused by Dragenlyte's obvious confusion than by the man driving the truck away. Then she put the pieces together and started after the truck, leaving Dragenlyte behind.

As Wurster now expected, the driver only moved the truck the one block to the other tubed traffic light pole - which happened to be on the far side of that cross-street. There the truck would block the view of much of what happened if she had stayed by the woman in the uniform of the thieves.

Wurster dialed the local number for the police on her cell phone as she walked, no need to run. The truck crew weren't done. They might hurry but she suspected wouldn't leave with just one of the old tubes.

With her camera and plenty of battery power for it, Wurster was delighted that where it stopped was one of the brighter spots because of the overhead lights along with the traffic lights.

As the driver was lowering the back ramp, she got into position to video tape it all with a clear view into the back of the truck.

When her phone call was answered, she said a few words into it, specifying where official intervention was needed. Done. Now she would prepare her statement to make the case against the thieves so the officers would have no doubts about what the needed to do.

She had seen enough of the first removal to not be surprised that there were two more men in the truck. She got a better look at their smooth operation as they removed the second tube.

Dragenlyte ran up and tried with limited success to block this stranger's view, and especially her camera view, with her hands.

Wurster had little trouble avoiding her.

"Stop. It's illegal for you to record the removal of items that have State approval to be moved," Dragenlyte called as she pulled out and waved a sheet of paper.

"Baloney? Hold that up and hold it still so I can see and record it if that's what that is. I don't believe you."

"I don't want to have to call the police to deal with you, but I will if you don't hand over that camera immediately."

"I've saved you the trouble. I've already called the police. We'll let them decide whether your paper means anything."

The three men were lowering the second removed tube so they could carry it onto the truck where a second pile of mats awaited it.

Suddenly, Wurster thought of something, turned and ran back the way she had come. Therefore, to Dragenlyte's relief the loading of the second tube into the truck was not video taped.

But things did change fast.

Wurster drove her car up and parked it within inches of the truck to block its forward path. Not even enough maneuver-around-the-car distance. It could of course easily push her car out of the way, but that would end the pretense of innocence of the theft.

And the local police car drove up, lights flashing but no siren, and parked behind and almost touching the truck. By then the ramp had been raised so it was even that bit closer. The three men got in the cab of the truck and settled to let the lady who hired them handle this.

Wurster, with her camera, hurried up to stand near Dragenlyte as Adrian Bleacher, opened the door and slowly got out.

He wore blue trousers and a shirt suggesting a uniform but with no patches on it - but had a badge on the shirt pocket. He moved slowly since he was paging almost frantically through a binder of papers marked: *Procedures While On Patrol*.

Wurster gawked; Dragenlyte smiled. It was amateur night in the Town of Festivity.

"Who are you?" Wurster asked Bleacher as she looked over and taped a view of the police car. It looked like one of the town's.

"My name's Officer Bleacher, Ma'am. I'm a new part-timer with the department. First night on the job in fact."

"Is there anyone else on duty at this time?" Wurster asked.

Dragenlyte wanted to know the same thing but was happy to have the other woman collect the information about this situation.

"No, Ma'am. But I have numbers I can call and who's on patrol duty in any of three nearby towns can come and help. Since there's no crash or fire I shouldn't need them. What's the problem here. Whoever called said tubes were being stolen but that doesn't make sense."

Wurster moaned; Dragenlyte had to fight not to dance for joy.

"The three men in the truck plus her loaded the two wooden tubes that belong to the town and should be around the traffic light poles into this truck to steal them. Arrest them for that. I'm the witness and I have a lot of it tape recorded," Wurster said.

Bleacher looked at the traffic light pole and shook his head. "I'm new here in town so I don't know what you mean by tubes that would fit around the traffic light poles. Are you sure about that description?"

Dragenlyte said, "Don't bother about that. All you need to know, Officer, sir, is that we have a permit from the State to do what we did. This is all simply delaying us getting things where they're to go now."

"She has a paper she says is that State permit but wouldn't let me see it. You should verify that," Wurster said.

"Let's move this along before you get in bad trouble for wasting time on your first night on duty, Officer. As a special friend of the chief I'll see to that. Here's the important document," Dragenlyte said as she held out a different sheet of paper.

"What is this, please?" Bleacher asked as he looked at the typed page with a scrawled signature at the bottom trying to make sense of it while trying to see it in his flashlight beam to read at all.

"It's a receipt for items I bought as representative of a company signed by a man who assured me he had the full authority to agree to sales of any and all Town of Festivity assets," Dragenlyte said.

"There's no company name or amount on here. And it only lists *assets of the town* as what was *released*. Doesn't say *sold*." Bleacher said.

"If you're not a lawyer that might seem light on detail but I can assure you that I've been told it's all legal," Dragenlyte said.

"Carefully worded so you can't say that she said it was legal, only that she was told so by persons unknown. That's why it's critical that you get her identity. Check your book on how," Wurster said.

"This is all more that I can deal with and since it's technical stuff I can't even call for help," Bleacher said.

Wurster grabbed the supposed receipt from him and held it to see the signature. "Signed by Nicholas Nickelby? He's not from here. He's a nobody. He has no authority to sneeze on any town property, much less sell it. Or release it. You, chief of the thieves, how much did he pay and who did you transfer the money to?"

"None of your business but he swore before witnesses that he had the necessary authority. I will tell you he was paid in cash so if the locals want to fuss, let them talk to him," Dragenlyte said.

Seeing motion in a parked car down the cross-street, Wurster scrutinized the spot through her video camera with the Zoom function. She could see the man sitting in a parked car that she recognized.

"That's Knuckles down there watching us. The last resort liar to back you up?" she asked Dragenlyte.

Bleacher shined his flashlight down there for something to do.

Dragenlyte waved to the driver, who started the truck motor.

Bleacher jumped in the police car and pulled back and out of the way to park and write up his required report.

Wurster hurried to stand on the far side of her car, handbag on the hood within reach.

The truck driver sneered out at Wurster as he prepared to put the truck in gear - but wiped that off his face and carefully backed the truck when she took what looked like a handgun from her handbag and waited for him to be stupid.

He backed to the corner, turned smoothly and headed out of town - with Dragenlyte in her car - and Knuckles in his - following.

Wurster moved her car so it wasn't blocking traffic, of which there was none, then sat in her car making notes for several minutes.

She never even noticed the police car drive away.

*　*　*

At 9 A.M. Wurster reported the nights happenings to Fred Quade. He in turn called a town committee meeting for 10 A.M.

Wurster was not a member, but attended as the only witness to the events who could be found.

Adrian Bleacher turned in his badge after his shift, said he quit, and could not be located. Speculation about whether he was paid off or was too ashamed by his poor first time performance was inevitable.

By then Wurster had searched the gang leader's car license number through the State motor vehicle records and identified her as one Sally Dragenlyte with an address in the big city.

She had also lifted several sets of the woman's fingerprints off the exterior of that car in case the Quades wanted to prove she touched things in their kitchen.

She told of the claim of State permission in writing to let the woman in complete robber wear do whatever she was doing. She would leave it to them to check if such a document had ever been issued . And of the receipt full of fakery. Both alleged documents waved around but not allowed to be verified.

To her disappointment but not surprise, no one wanted to file charges and try to have the woman who seemed to be in charge of what happened arrested. There was agreement that there was not enough benefit for a lot of expensive legal hassle.

Only a few knew there were a second set of tubes in storage. The sets were made together so that if the first ones were damaged during filming of early scenes that wouldn't slow up the filming of the rest.

Febrraro, Quade, and others quietly replaced them and, after the tubes being gone only one morning, few realize what had happened.

Knuckles was known to be about to leave the town anyway and he was gone at dawn. Two days later his body was found in another State, dead in a car crash. High blood alcohol, no cash or anything else except a few clothes found with him.

Only the connection between the Collector who wanted - and presumably received - the movie set tubes, and the town drunk who was willing to advise on a scam and sign papers claiming authority he didn't have would ever know how long her profit from all of this would keep Dragenlyte going.

Chapter 06

Ms. Dragenlyte didn't usually pay attention to the little people filler bits on the local TV news programs but was happy she had been distracted and therefore slow to click away in this case.

There was Toby Jansen being interviewed as part of a panel at his high school. She had ignored the lead in to this point but focused when he named three colleges he had heard were good schools to have a degree from. The interviewer promptly asked the next student on the panel whether she planned to go to college.

In short order, the TV was off and she was busy making notes on her laptop. This was an opening to mess things up for that brat without being open about it.

Yes, there was pleasure in taking credit for your subtle actions but if others judged those too mean or sneaky you risked doing yourself more harm than any short-lived personal glee was worth if identified as involved. This unexpected opening was a chance to be sneaky that she almost instantly planned in her head, Only she would know she had a literal hand in it but she would rejoice at the long-term damage she did that uncooperative kid.

He hadn't been asked if he hoped or planned to attend any of the schools he named but that was little reason to believe that he said that and was determined to make it happen.

By what was finally paying off as a lucky chance, she recently took a few minutes and delivered a bag of groceries to a man currently in barely functional medical state whom she had learned was related to people it might benefit her to impress. She only carried in the bag, handed it off to the paid caregiver, introduced herself and spoke a few bland words to the patient on the hope that he might react in some way when her name was mentioned later by those she wanted to impress. She could not think of any other subtle way to get that message out.

Until she saw that TV report, she had barely noted that patient Cameron Poe had the same name as a man of current fame but she hadn't checked for what. In fact. he was a character in a movie of some box office note. Suddenly though, that name was the critical piece for her scheme to keep the Jansen brat from the colleges of his dreams.

She found an app to create letterhead stationery and inserted his name as Ranger Cameron Poe and his real mail address but no phone number or a web address.

She composed letters to the Admissions Office of the three schools Toby had named. She identified him by name and mailing address, which was as much as she knew about him. The letters warned that this young man was a known cheater and was planning to cause trouble on campus if accepted - without offering any verification or sources for the claims.

She mailed those to the colleges with the supposed writer's name but not a return address on the envelopes. She wanted the name to trigger automatic acceptance that would tamp down any suspicions.

All she needed to do now was intercept any responses from the colleges. Doable, since his residence had a curbside mail box.

* * *

Probably Drag had not noticed Klemper before but Klemper had noted her on three occasions and concluded she was a sneaky kiss-up never to be trusted.

Dragenlyte arrived a bit late at the birthday party for a social biggie thrown by his family in a hotel ballroom. She made a walk around trying without much success to work the room. Most guests were gathered in eight groups of about six each, each group talking about a main topic. Another dozen including her, were working the room or being ignored, some resenting that, some reveling in it.

Dragenlyte wanted to join a group. But which one? Only one group was talking standard celebrity gossip fluff. The others were updating one another in fairly serious fashion about the group's topic. If you pushed into one of the groups you had better be ready to hold your own and contribute to the details of the topic. Show your ignorance and be soundly rejected.

Her solution to which to join was to spy by proxy. Buy ears of a server who was moving between groups but staying in each while handing out finger foods and drinks and collecting glasses.

Several servers were reluctant to talk to her except business lest they be called out for overstepping. Klemper would talk.

Dragenlyte said, "As a favor to me, can you please tell me what you've managed to hear is the topic each group is focused on?"

"It's not my job to listen, only to serve, Ma'am."

Dragenlyte got it. "Of course I'd make worth a server's time."

"Worth it by how much?"

Drag was surprised by the blatant question but said, "Twenty dollars if I think it's useful information."

"Dat's not enough to risk a hassle with the caterer for talking too much mit any guest. Und it vould be for sure, not if you den decide to come up with it. "I can tell about six of der groups for eine hundred dollars. Dis is der money crowd so der help is not for cheapniks."

"Agreed"

"From der left as dey stand. Celebrity gossip, fluff. Medical insurance, Der Broadway shows, who played der parts. Medical procedures and equipment as der investments. Der new tell-all book about der president. Und horse racing. But a caution on that last."

"I don't need the likes of you to tell me how to pass and sell myself," Dragenlyte said, waved Klemper back to serving.

First Dragenlyte checked out the investing group but backed away since they were talking over her head.

On another pass, Klemper asked for her money but she was waved off with, "That was a joke, not a commitment to a *servant*."

She was braced for an unpleasant moment but knew she had the advantage since the server would be blackballed for that, not herself. She was relieved - with just a tinge of concern that the woman seemed to accept her loss too easily.

Dragenlyte went to join the horse racing group expecting to impress two people she has identified by name and who might be useful to have as backers.

She too eagerly spouted some bad info and was openly laughed out of the group who were all serious and knowledgeable about blood lines.

Thoroughly embarrassed, Dragenlyte hurried to leave before too many around the room identified her.

When she passed Klemper, who was calmly watching and shrugging, Dragenlyte verbally attacked her - although quietly so as not to attract attention of others.

"What did you set me up for?"

"I tried to caution you. I tried to warn that they were experts and you needed to be too to join them. You said you didn't need to know anything from der *servant*, so too bad for you. And don't be kidding yourself, the word will spread and soon everyone will be laughing at you and fixing you in their minds as not one of them."

Then Klemper walked away from Dragenlyte, not the reverse.

* * *

Fiftyish Mrs. Hohum stopped on the urban street to turn back to shout an insult at the large man who had come barreling along the pavement at her determined to get where he intended as fast as he could without running and everybody else had best get out of his way.

She was one of the everybody elses and had the good sense to step almost into the street to let him by. Then she put down her tote bag of groceries, turned, and once she felt sure he was too far away to come back to have words with her, shouted her outrage after him.

When she then refocused on her groceries, two things grabbed her attention. First, her tote bag had fallen over and a loaf of bread and a plastic jar of mayonnaise were very near the curb. Two, a moving car was very close to her and her groceries.

She stepped aside, inadvertently kicking the bag so those items were pushed off the curb and crushed by the car tires without the driver being able to see that happening.

Outrage heaped on outrage! Mrs. Hohum looked for someone to blame for this. And there, ambling along after coming around the corner so he had seen none of that, came Shane Pawling.

Mrs. Hohum stepped in front of him as she waved her arms, twice having to dodge her own large handbag that was on her arm. She shouted, "You. You must have done it. You should be arrested and not allowed on the public streets."

Coming toward her from the other direction, Toby shouted at her, "Tell everybody what you say he did? You look silly and like the one who shouldn't be allowed on the public streets without a minder."

Several passers-by stopped to watch this and two to record it themselves. Hohum was confused by this stranger's intrusion.

Toby kept a straight face during that, which made many of the others in the area think he was making simple common sense. Their silent reactions also said, *Make your case but be specific.*

Mrs. Hohum stopped and looked around befuddled. This was not what she intended to happen. She was a wronged person, therefore somebody, this young man would do, needed to be blamed. Now he had joined the dozen people who had stopped to watch this, waiting for her to make her case.

"I put down my bag of groceries and he knocked it over and things fell out and got run over by a car," she finally said.

"Are you saying he meant to do that, if he did?" Toby asked.

"Well I say he should have been more careful. The police should have a talk with him," she said, determined to stand her ground.

"Do you want to call a cop? I see one up the block," Toby said.

As she considered that, Toby held up his cell phone so three of those who stopped to witness this could see a video clip on there. They all looked at Mrs. Hohum and shook their heads. No, she was wrong.

Toby stepped over and showed the clip to Shane and several others who crowded closer eager to see it.

"You're not a judge to say what's right," she said defensively.

"But I am the person with the evidence that the judge would have to consider since it shows the whole thing. I saw you have to get out of the way of that pushy man and started to record you. By luck I had the right angle to see you accidentally kick over your own bag, resulting in that mayonnaise sandwich in the street."

"I say he did it. That's my right. You can't stop me, I'm gonna report him to the police."

"Not even gonna try to stop you," Toby said. "But my video is the evidence for his counter law suit to empty your vacation fund when you do. But, hey, you'll be probably be on the news gossip items section three times. When you file the erroneous report; when a court rules against you; and when the court awards him your money. But it might work the other way since you're sure you have the facts right with only your word as evidence."

Mrs. Hohum angrily waved Shane on his way and he walked on as a local TV news crew ran up to interview her - while Toby stood nearby ready to intervene.

To the TV camera, she blamed passing cars making the street vibrate and denounced the city for not fixing that. Laughter all around.

She fled, being called by name since already identified.

*　*　*

A short time later, Toby stood with items at the checkout of a nearby convenience store patting his pockets and blushing when he remembered he had no money on him.

"I'm so sorry. I only expected to drop something into a corner mailbox and go back inside but I thought of... I'll shut up now. Sorry that you have to make the register..."

Shane walked by, wordlessly holding out a ten dollar bill.

Toby saw who it was, took the money, and handed it to the clerk, saying, "It's good to have friends who aren't as scatterbrained as me." He reached for other items on a display. "That should be enough for these too. I'll share what he paid for with him as my thanks."

*　*　*

Minutes later Toby and Shane sat on a bench in an urban pocket park with the newly purchased munchies between them

"Yeah, the clerks's expression was wonderful. She was happier that I was - and I was darned happy - to have an apparent total stranger simply offer me money to pay what she had rung up," Toby said.

"Sort of like I was that you and your phone were the right place to deal with that mayonnaise sandwich. I saw how many people laughed when you called it that."

"We've gotten comfortable and learned to just do what's needed without a lot of chit chat up front in the four years we've known one another. We don't live far apart but never met until high school."

"Soon we'll both be college guys, polishing ourselves up to make the world a better place," Shane said.

"But at least to start off we'll both be living at home. Do you have work for the summer?"

"Part-time at two places. Stock man. More brawn than brains."

"But if the job only needs your basic attention, you can work on other stuff in your head. Maybe making notes on a pocket notebook."

"Gotta be ready for the quick move that helps you or your buddy out of sticky situation," Shane said. "I'm thinking of when that man in the park was hassling you about stealing his wallet and I threw a stick at him from behind the statue and hit him."

"He started over to see who threw the stick and saw his wallet on the ground where he threw it when he turned real fast to check on a noise as he was trying to put it in his back pocket. Too proud to admit his mistake, but he blushed as he grabbed it up and hurried away."

"Or the anonymous message I left on her phone machine telling that woman where to look for the package you had left outside her door but the neighbor's dog had then carried over behind a bush. Lucky she had a listed number," Shane said.

"Saved me trying to explain what happened to it since you saw that as you went by but I was long gone. Ever since I ask myself when an anonymous phone call might be the fastest solution to a problem."

"Oops, time flies when I'm munching goodies. Time to go stock some shelves."

"Me too. Good to see you. Feel free to use the books in our shed but please don't take them away 'til I'm sure I'm done with 'em."

* * *

The members and invited guests-only annual meeting of the Lady Keepers of the Fire Social Club at the country club was a kind of event Ms. Dragenlyte would not pass up simply because she didn't meet the entrance requirements.

She simply parked in the far lot and avoided the gate-keepers by walking around to the back of the building and joining those on the veranda acting like she belonged. She didn't plan to stay for the meal - when they might again check identities - she intended to beg off to go attend to critical business after she made herself known to those she judged based on short observation to be true movers and therefore worth cultivating.

She was startled but tried to hide that when Klemper came over and offered her a drink from her tray, saying quietly, "You should avoid der problem here vhere you don't know der peoples."

Dragenlyte was taking a first measure of the group and had not paid attention to this woman in a server's uniform. She now recognized her - and assumed she was hinting that she could warn her about who had already identified her as a party crasher.

"Get away. I don't need anything at all from you."

Klemper nodded and walked away as if she had offered the guest a beverage and the guest declined.

A moment later two women standing near Dragenlyte began to shout loud abuse and one another - then they stormed off in different directions.

Two other women hurried to Dragenlyte and asked in urgent whispers what she said to those others that set them off like that. Their tone said that they were blaming her for causing the fuss and that they intended to penalize her for that once they were certain.

Dragenlyte was shocked, outraged - and relieved. She could honestly say she hadn't said a word to those two. She also could read the disbelief on the faces of these two. She needed reinforcement.

Dragenlyte pointed after Klemper and said, "I was asking that server something, I didn't say a word to those others or even that they could overhear."

Those woman waved over Klemper and asked what she had been talking to Dragenlyte about. Klemper said she had offered her a beverage, the newly arrived guest declined so she went off to see if anyone else needed anything. The guest said no more to her.

By then several others had stepped over to find out what was going on. Before Dragenlyte could react two women took phone pics of her so she could not slip away as a mystery person.

It was clear that the common opinion was that Dragenlyte was a liar and there were questions about her not wearing a name badge she should have been given at the door.

What should she do now? What *could* she do now?

As more people gathered to hear about the new situation, Klemper acted as though she saw someone signaling to her from across the veranda. She pointed to Dragenlyte with a questioning gesture, then nodded and stepped to Dragenlyte. She said loudly enough for others to hear, "Ma'am, there is a phone call for you inside. I can take you where you need to go."

Dragenlyte was glad to follow and more relieved than she wanted to have show that no one tried to block them.

Inside, Klemper led Dragenlyte and pointed to a landline phone, then turned her back to give her privacy for her call.

Relieved to have escaped the club members but confused about this call, Dragenlyte lifted the phone - and heard the dial tone.

Klemper rolled her eyes as the other stared - then finally got that the supposed call was her rescue. She could slip out and to her car and hope she took such bad phone photos that no one would be able to positively identify her.

Klemper said, "For me not saving you inside, you only do what profits you and I'm following your example. Pay attention."

When Dragenlyte didn't promptly move, Klemper help out her hand, gesturing to be paid.

Dragenlyte got the idea now and put some cash in that hand.

Klemper let her look show how disappointed and dissatisfied she was with that amount.

When Dragenlyte put more money in her hand, Klemper pointed to a door she could use to slip away now.

Chapter 07

Even in her secret never to be shared with anyone notes on her laptop, Sally Dragenlyte never admitted out loud, much less in writing, how much the thrill of risky ventures excited her. She discovered this about herself at an early age and periodically tested her limits.

Today was such a test. Her fixation for nasty satisfaction at this time was messing things up for Toby Jansen's plans for college.

She had sent the fake letters to what she believed were his main choices and was eager to know his reactions to being rejected but could not risk going through the Jansen household incoming mail.

Then she suspected what she wanted to know would be on his computer. Spying on him twice when she had nothing important to do and got some satisfaction from being an undiscovered snoop, she saw him carrying what was likely a laptop. Surely that would contain all she wanted to know - and if he lost that it would make everything harder for him and that would please her.

So here she was wearing a simple disguise. A second-hand store black wide-brimmed hat with a full veil with neatly pressed navy blue sweats, the fancy brand labels cut out as if that would convince anyone who saw her, and no one was supposed to, that it was somebody poor sneaking around.

Her destination was the Jansen's backyard shed where she had once heard his mother say Toby worked on hobbies and projects. The shed's door was only steps from the back fence so you could sneak close and hurry to and through the door when no Jansens were in sight.

She got inside - only thinking as she was out in the open that the door might be locked - but it wasn't.

She stopped when she pulled the door closed behind her. Anyone here to surprise her? She was playing this by ear so she would decide whether to run for it or stay and talk her way thorough it once she could see who and what were where.

Nobody was obvious although an overhead light was on. She thought no more about that because she could see a laptop on a shelf under the worktable that was the main furniture.

She examined the laptop in silence, thinking it looked well worn so he must not have the good sense to take care of his possessions.

That pleased her since it hinted that he might not even miss it for a day or two. She had come with the intent of taking it with her rather than staying here where some family member could walk in and find her at any moment while she was fumbling around trying to download files onto a data stick, however you did that.

With a nod and a smile, she put the computer into the tote bag she had brought in under her shirt even if it made her look fat.

She almost lost control of the tote and of several body systems when a deep voice said, "Put that back and step away from it."

It was Shane Pawling. He had been working in another corner when she came in. As she examined the laptop, he donned a Halloween Darth Vader full head mask and cape over a distinctive shirt with lightning going into a cartoon skull and *An Amazing Idea Sponge* printed below, then stepped out to confront her. From phone pics that Toby had shown over time he was pretty sure he knew who she was but hoped she couldn't identify him.

After an initial gasp, she decided she could win here by being the more aggressive one. She said, "I didn't take anything."

"Then leave the tote bag and get out," he said.

"I don't think you can make me do that."

"Think about the consequences if you're wrong." He did sound like he wanted to get aggressive now.

"I'm going to take it because I have permission to do so."

"No, you don't." As he said that he shoved a movable worktable over to block them both from the only door.

"I can do whatever I want with this," she said hefting the tote.

His response was to adjust the movable table to better block the door. Then he spun around, picked up a smartphone from where he had been working, and faced her again as he tapped keys on that.

"You have no say, you don't live here," she insisted.

"Hello, Nine-One-One Operator. What is your emergency?"

He said into the phone, "There is a robbery in progress here by a dragon lady in a silly big hat and veil disguise that'll make her obvious from two blocks away."

She sneered, sure he had faked the call - but maybe wondering how he did the radio voice.

"As for that dragon lady comment, buster..."

She literally jumped a foot and almost fainted when a police car siren started no more that two blocks away.

She banged down the laptop on the main worktable, hoping to damage it, and grumbled fierce threats as Shane kept the movable table between them but let her escape with her bag before cops arrived.

On her way out the door, Dragenlyte passed the startled Louise Jansen, holding her own smartphone, who was sure she recognized her and called her by name.

Louise didn't know exactly what had happened here but she had suspicions about the kind of thing that might have. Shane quickly filled her in on what had been attempted but thwarted as she nodded that she understood and thought it was something like that.

While he did that, he sent a copy of the video of Dragenlyte sneaking in the door from his phone to hers.

She said, "Be quick, Shane. Don't argue and don't talk about this to anyone until we can talk later. Put the costume where you found it. Leave me your shirt. Toby's on that shelf should fit you well enough for now. Get out of here fast as I delay the police so they won't see you. "

Louise hurried outside and to the street. Shane did those things and went out and into the neighbor's yard and away from there.

Shane was safely gone when Louise led two cops inside.

She pointed to the laptop on the worktable and said, "A person unknown tried to steal my son's laptop. I came out to get that shirt to put in the wash load and surprised him or her. I'm hesitant about this since I can't rule out that it might have been a set up for a teenager practical joke."

She slid the movable table more out of the way as she assessed the officers' reactions to her suggestion. They seemed open to it.

"The person was wearing an outlandish veiled hat that begged you to notice him or her. I got only a passing view and with the veil can't ID him or her. Since the computer's still here I won't ask that the police to do more than file a report for now. My son needs to check if anything else that was here is gone."

Soon then they were gone, the paperwork taken care of.

Louise held up Shane's shirt and said, "Didn't have to mention you, Shane, but you're part of the twist. I'll confuse Sally about who she dealt with by washing this shirt with its distinctive design that she only saw on you and put it out on the dryer in the yard. Maybe even leave it there overnight to taunt her. She'll drive by looking for hints of who's knows what and will keep coming to a conclusion she's sure can't be correct. She tries to sneak close for a better look, the motion sensor turns on the outside lights - and she wets herself."

* * *

This fast food place was a convenient place for Toby and Shane to meet without being recognized since neither had been here before.

"I know it was scary. I owe you triple for defending my stuff."

"I never would have been there if I knew she'd show up," Shane said with a shudder at the thought of being so close to the Dragon Lady.

"We're almost sure it was her but none of my family expected her to come there. I think it was her mistake too. It only makes sense to me if she thought that that was my main laptop with all my up to date stuff on there," Toby said.

"I risked her wrath to save a useless machine?!"

"Calm down. We don't want to attract attention. It's not useless, but it is my old one with little trade-in value that I only do some online research on. If it gets a virus, at least the damage is contained."

"You mentioned her before and showed me some pics so I knew who she was but I wasn't prepared for how nasty she seems. And the threats she made to me. They scared me then and still do now."

"That's why I wanted to talk to you as soon as we could arrange it. To thank you - and also to tell you that my mom never mentioned you to the police for their report. Then she washed your shirt and put it outside to dry so it seems like it's mine. Do you see what that means?"

"That you're stealing my shirt?"

"Not quite. It means the dragon lady doesn't know you exist."

Shane wasn't sure he followed that.

"She thought it was me in the costume mom said you had on - which I wore last Halloween if Aunt Sally can check around."

"She doesn't know I even exist!" Shane said happily as he got it.

"One thing we should agree to is that I pay you for that shirt so I can wear it in public now and then to keep reinforcing that it was me in the shed, not some guy she hasn't identified yet."

"I really like that shirt but that's a small price for being wiped from her radar."

"I hoped you'd agree. And mom is pissed with her cousin but has agreed not to press charges for the break-in, which legally it was."

* * *

At the social gathering in the hotel ballroom before the major company's business meeting Dragenlyte went to Klemper, working the event, thanked her for her rescue at the country club, and asked for her help at this event. On silent cue, Klemper would bring a new type of smartphone from a product display to Dragenlyte who would would have set up a company exec to be impressed by her business acumen. Her points about that item would then add her to that woman's circle of influencers. For $200, paid in cash in advance.

Klemper agreed and pocketed the money, then said that it was important to be careful not to mention that item to certain people. Dragenlyte shushed her and sent her away as she saw her target moving to where she could intercept her. She was a pro and didn't need advice from Klemper on who to butter up and use.

In short order, Dragenlyte chatted up her target and waved over Klemper with the demo new phone.

Even faster Dragenlyte was denounced by many people all around for her sick joke. Not having done nearly enough research on her, Dragenlyte was trying to interest this woman whose family had lost big money on an investment in a similar device that failed badly. That mistake wrecked the family company, her parents' marriage, and their mental health. Using a legally changed name she had been building a career on her own, with most going to some trouble not to refer back to the disaster she had nothing to do with. Now this.

Dragenlyte prudently fled the scene, glad she hadn't talked to many others so her name might not become widely known.

Later Dragenlyte met in private with Klemper and they agreed to work together. Klemper would be salaried as an assistant, no longer dependent on iffy jobs with caterers. They mutually agreed that neither did or likely ever would totally trust the other.

* * *

Dragenlyte checked the curbside mailbox outside Cameron Poe's house for incoming mail daily. It was a bit of trouble but minimal since he had to have mail opened and read to him at present and had hired someone to do that only on Sunday afternoons. Between Sundays the few pieces of mostly junk mail simply accumulated in the box.

Over several days she intercepted form letters from each of those colleges thanking Mr. Poe for his interest. Those convinced her that she has screwed Toby's big plans.

The day she picked up the third letter she was confronted by a man who identified himself as Mr. Poe's lawyer. He took the unopened response letter from her and asked what she knew about a letter to one of the other colleges that Mr. Poe had supposedly sent.

She claimed no knowledge of such a letter but he clearly did not believe her. From then, she was barred from entering his house or taking the mail from the curbside box. Poe had at times given her generous amounts of cash for small tasks she told him she did for him but hadn't. Now that source of cash was gone.

She returned the next week and and found a guard dog and a maid who didn't find her intimidating blocking her access to the house and the mailbox. And daring her to make a fuss..

She told herself that messing up Toby was worth that loss but didn't believe it. She added this to her list of grievances against him.

* * *

Toby stood talking away on his smartphone close to the edge of the curb at an intersection through two cycles of the lights.

Still distracted, he almost stepped into the street when the light gave the waiting cars the go-ahead to be in that space - except that Shane, approaching him on his own chore, wordlessly picked Toby up, turned 360, put him down, and walked up the cross-street as Toby focused on his near disaster.

Observers are fascinated that both were casual doing that.

* * *

Wary but not afraid, Toby agreed to walk with Mrs. Gordon.

She led the way along an alley behind a block of old factory buildings on each side, all the windows in sight bricked up.

"Sorry, I know this seems extreme and it probably is but my husband and I are trained to always think about watchers and listeners. There's no real danger in this case but could be some fuss. My husband and I have to be away for several days on short notice. For about thirty hours Mrs, Norton who usually care of our children when we're not home won't be available."

Toby nodded that he understood this so far.

"I don't know how much your parents have told you about what they think we do."

"They say you work for the government. Diplomatic work is what they call it. I get that it's not stuff you can talk about much," he said.

"Good enough for our purposes today. That work means we have to be extra careful about hiring people to do anything in our condo and especially anything involving our children."

He nodded that that made sense.

"We're sort of in a time bind. We need someone to be in charge of the three kids until Mrs. Norton can get back. We'd appreciate it if you could do this for us."

Toby smiled. This sounded like something he could handle.

Mrs. Gordonwent on, "Two points before you answer. I asked your parents if it was okay to ask you. They both said they're confident you're good for the responsibility.

He smiled and nodded, happy to hear that.

"And you're just over the age line so they won't be home alone with you there but there will also be an older woman who'll stay with the four of you the whole time in case something happens and someone older needs to sign papers or take over. We all refer to her as Mrs. Smith. She's quiet and won't try to take charge unless things get very scary fast. This'll be a much deserved rest break for her."

"I'd be happy to help out - and to have a chance to get to know my cousins. I'm not a trained sitter but I learn fast," Toby said.

"That's wonderful but I won't hold you to it yet. There's one more important element to the story."

Toby let his concern about what this might be show.

"There are written orders barring your aunt Sally from visiting the condo while we're away. We'll leave a phone number for you. One call at any hour or location will bring people running ready and eager to remove her despite any fuss from her. I know from your mother that you've had some interactions with your aunt."

"Oh yes. But none that scare me off if I know there's backup."

"We're worried about her being too snoopy and too apt to do things that will give others openings to search our apartment as part of investigating what she seemed to be doing there. We don't trust her not to tell those she's trying to impress insider information that she might overhear or snoop out. Her loose lip could put us on the news and make our work harder or impossible." She stopped, worried that she had lost control and made too much fuss.

"I'll get satisfaction from keeping her away until Mrs. Norton gets back," he said.

"Mrs. Norton is by now a master at guarding the doors."

Chapter 08

Toby was confused to get a rejection letter from one of the three schools warned about him by someone named Cameron Poe.

He emailed them and asked what that was about since he hadn't applied there. He suggested they check on who was hoaxing them and why, hinting that them being faked out would be news headlines.

*   *   *

At the science museum Toby and the Gordon kids walked by some machine exhibits acknowledging that those items were important but not that exciting to the kids yet.

Cindy, at not yet five; Victor, at a bit beyond eight; and Marla who was approaching eleven, found the animal diorama exhibits more interesting since between them they could name many of the types. They had seen the species in photos and videos but never before in the preserved skin and bones to really grasp their sizes.

Toby was surprised that they had never been to a zoo but Marla explained that away as scheduling problems with the many other things they were taken to experience. He got them more interested by noting body adaptations of several animals and described behavior quirks of a few types and challenging them to point out others.

*   *   *

This was the first time the Gordon kids ever ate lunch bought from street food carts. They liked it as a change of pace even if there was a limited menu where they were. Hot dogs and bottled beverages at one cart; ice cream at another. They saw a truck with a wider menu but were happier with the simple meal this time.

Then, since they were in no hurry, Toby walked them several more blocks to show them the fuller picture that you didn't have to find a restaurant for lunch in center city. And when you felt adventurous you could sample a variety of ethnic foods that way with little fuss.

Mrs. Smith stayed in the background but alert. To the degree that she showed any reactions to them, she approved of their day out.

* * *

At the Gordon condo that evening, dinner was in the fridge ready to be heated in the microwave. Toby pretended relief and Victor exaggerated that - as Marla assured Carla they were both kidding.

"Victor, please set the table while this heats," Toby said.

"No way. That's girls' work," Victor said and folded his arms across his chest. His sisters looked at him with disapproval but waiting to see how Toby would handle this.

Toby leaned toward the boy and said in a stage whisper, "Sorry, kiddo. I didn't realize you don't know how to do that and don't want us to see your embarrassment. It's really simple. I'm sure Marla will be nice and tutor you about it later if you want. We'll pretend not to be laughing at you right now while you try to hide behind a dumb excuse."

Victor was stricken. He stared, jaw hanging open in disbelief.

Then Marla started to applaud - so Carla joined in although she wasn't sure why they were doing that.

"I can do it, I was just…"

"Checking that I was paying attention. I realize that. Thanks for keeping me alert," Toby said.

Victor started to put the dishes around the table. When Marla stepped over to help, he waved her off. He could do this if he chose to.

Marla looked to Toby who winked at her. She smiled and went to get silverware from a drawer.

* * *

Later, they agreed they wanted to watch a DVD movie but each child had favorites and couldn't decide on which to view again.

He had brought three with him that were all new to them and that all would probably enjoy. A fast learner, he only mentioned and showed them one of those. When they all showed some enthusiasm for that, he put that one to go into the player, then slipped the others into his backpack not to be mentioned this evening.

As they all settled on the sofa facing the TV screen, Victor said to Toby, "You seem like an old man,"

"Thank you for noticing. I seem to be more aware of things since someone might be trying to mess things up for me. I'm glad to know I don't seem as out of it as I try to pretend at times. And no, I won't explain what's going on since it's aimed at me but if you go mentioning it you might get targeted too. Plus, that's not a fun talk subject which if what I want to have with you guys today."

"What did mom tell you to do about Aunt Sally?" Marla asked.

"Not to let her in - and not to talk about her," Toby answered.

"But she's for real," Carla said.

"Yes, but it's easier to try not to think about her. Like maybe she's only imaginary. Like a yeti," Toby said.

"What's a yeti?" Victor let Carla asked for them both.

"A so-called abominable snowman said to live high up in the Himalaya mountains. They've been talked about as real for a long time but not a single one has ever been found to prove they are," Toby said.

"Like Bigfoot," Marla said.

"Correct. Bigfoot, also called a Sasquatch, is a legendary creature that supposedly lives up in Washington State and Canada. Same deal, occasional reports of sightings but no proven ones. And a bunch that we know were faked. Even been movies with them as characters."

"I wanna see tonight's movie now," Carla said.

"Me too," Toby said and started the player.

*　*　*

Toby choose to sleep in a sleeping bag he brought with him on the master bedroom floor. He didn't discuss it with anyone else, just didn't feel right using the bed although told he could.

In the morning, the young Gordans came in and woke him. At least he played it that way. "Morning already? You kids wore me out."

Marla whispered to him, "I think you're faking that."

"Maybe so, maybe not. Does it really make any difference?"

"Why pretend about it? She persisted.

"To have a little time to think about stuff that's important to me before I have to focus on practical stuff like making breakfast," he said. "Do the three of you like waffles?"

"We like them okay, not a total favorite. But I know there are none in the freezer," Marla said.

"But I checked the pantry yesterday and saw a waffle iron and mix and eggs in the fridge. Everything except syrup," he said.

"I know where that is," she said. "Mom keeps it on a high shelf so we won't make a mess with it."

"I suspect there's a story behind that, but I won't pry," Toby said as Marla giggled and blushed.

They enjoyed the freshly made waffles with syrup. All agreed that the ones to be heated in the toaster were convenient and didn't need a bowl and various implements to make but that it was fun to do the work of making them every once in a while to remind themselves that they could. Especially with a dishwasher available.

Mrs. Norton arrived shortly after noon to take over so Toby packed his few things to go and catch up on things elsewhere.

At Victor's instigation, the three kids made a fuss about being so happy that Mrs. Norton was finally there to rescue them from bad jokes and not being spoiled. Then all laughed.

*　*　*

In the store where Toby was working part-time stocking shelves, Klemper, as always required to walk behind Dragenlyte and act like they were not together, saw a head-high wall of unopened cartons waiting to be unpacked onto shelves.

There was walk-by space on both sides but few, and maybe not even store security cameras, could see what a person on the back side of those might do.

Having heard her new boss go on several times about how she wanted to make trouble for Toby Jansen, whom she recognized as that young employee, Klemper gestured subtly to Dragenlyte that if some of that carton wall fell forward, there would be a mess and Toby, as the only nearby person, would get blamed.

Nod of go-ahead.

Toby glanced over, saw and recognized Klemper as she scuttled behind the stacks of cartons in a manner too sneaky not to be noticed. He saw the carton wall move a bit as she tested if this could happen.

Toby quickly moved the platform truck stacked with cartons that he has been working off over and lined that up, moving it along as needed, so each time Klemper tried to push top cartons to fall forward, cartons on the platform truck keep them from doing so.

During this, he called on a no-hands store radio for help. That alert brought other employees running. Two of them stopped to record Klemper and her actions on their phones when they could see her.

Then store security arrived on the run to talk to her - as she watched Dragenlyte flee while Toby directed others to video her.

Nastiness foiled - and publicly recorded. Klemper made the local TV news that evening as an odd troublemaker not yet identified.

* * *

Days later, Shane fled a store where he was stocking shelves two days a week before college when he saw Dragenlyte enter the store.

She probably did not see him and had seen him only in the Darth Vader costume and a distinctive shirt so could not recognize him. But he didn't risk that.

Shane called Toby and Toby called a girl he knew who Shane saw deal with Dragenlyte. She simply made a small purchase while acting like she was the new queen of Sheba. Didn't look around or at people.

* * *

On an urban street, senior citizen Clark accused Shane of taking a grapefruit he was hand-carrying home from him since he couldn't find it and Shane was the only one passing by when he realized that.

Clark shouted and waved to a cop to deal with Shane (who had a bag of groceries - that did not include any grapefruits).

The cop arrived and Clark made his accusation.

Toby tapped the Cop's arm and pointed to a grapefruit and a cloth handkerchief on the ground nearby, but maybe where Clark could not see them.

The Cops pointed the items out to Clark without touching them. Before he wrote up an accusation that Shane took the fruit, he asked Clark how, once accused, Shane could put them there? Did Shane throw the fruit around the man? Clark admitted he couldn't imagine how Shane could have done that but he must have.

Then, gently questioned, he conceded he may have dropped the fruit when he felt a sneeze coming on and needed empty hands to get his handkerchief ready. Now he couldn't find that either.

The Officer pointed to both missing items on ground - as he tipped his cap to Toby and waved Shane on his way.

* * *

Toby was helping spread mulch among newly planted flowers in the beds of a public park. At the moment he was on his hands and knees on a paved area near the tilted up back of a small truck filled with the stuff as he gathered spilled mulch into a pile to move to the bed.

Klemper, carrying a large tote bag of collected cosmetic samples from a store promotion, trailed behind Dragenlyte, who struggled to look like someone important and above all those around her.

Klemper recognized Toby and stopped where he couldn't see her to consider the possibilities here.

When Dragenlyte glanced back to be sure the older woman was looking appropriately subservient, Klemper nodded at the young man - and the half-truck load of mulch - and wordlessly inquired whether it would amuse the boss to see him get messed up by being mulched on.

The wordless nod said yes.

Klemper moved closer and examined the hardware. You pulled down on a metal bar handle to raise the door at the top of a chute on the back edge of the truck to let mulch pour down the chute and into a wheelbarrow that right now was a few feet to the side. When released, a heavy spring helped close the door back down.

Klemper moved closer in a fake stumbling gait. She pretended to lose her balance. She grabbed and pushed down on the rod, which should send a deluge of damp mulch down over the startled Toby since it would all happen so fast.

At the last moment, Toby rolled aside. In the process he tripped Klemper so she really did fall down at that spot. And yes, pulling on the handle as she did so - and holding on for a few extra seconds in surprise - she was the one who ended under a sizable pile of moist mulch that stuck to her hair, clothes, and skin.

But that didn't end it. Toby recognized her and kept this going.

He jumped up, barely touched by mulch, and grabbed up the tote bag that Klemper had tossed aside to free her hand when she felt herself going down.

He looked into the bag, then looked around and spotted his aunt Sally.

He waved and called loudly, "Yoo-hoo, Ms. Dragenlyte, your servant tried to bury this bag full of free samples of skin care. Wow, you sure need a lot of them. Are you going to come and take them to keep them safe until you can slather them on and hope for some benefit?"

A small crowd had stopped to watch, several recording it on their phones. Ones who had seen the action from the start, were telling the late-comers what had happened. Dragenlyte fled.

During that Klemper worked her way out of the mess, slowing when she found the mulch slippery underfoot and a real danger.

She wanted to attack Toby - or at least point him out and shout abuse and accusations at him. But he had dropped the tote bag and walked away out of her sight, leaving her trying to clean herself up enough to walk safely while trying to figure out how to get home now since she had only a dollar in her pocket - and the other woman's tote bag of free samples.

Chapter 09

It needed to be done and done soon. Important things needed to be arranged and it was hard to estimate how long and how much it would take to set the traps so a simple little request that might end up having major diplomatic consequences could be done before the top of the line caterer was booked. Planting anonymous questions about nasty actions to his work for people of little consequence to her took time and care. A verified trace back to her and she would have to move to the Midwest, change her name, rewrite her biography, and try to start over.

First task was a schedule session with the calendar. She needed to plan things that would have to keep falling into place for months. It would be too easy to get distracted - but once she fell behind, it would all fail.

Then she would have to make the extra hard decisions about what to allow to fall flat as long as she could jump clear, too bad about those who would be disappointed. Especially the ones who did a lot of work for nothing if she stepped away because they didn't have her brass or skill at cajoling others to do the work but let her take the credit.

She had a list of four items.

Once the calendar of events was set - with the essential small but necessary amount of wiggle room - she then had to decide whether to inform the parents of her decision to help them out or to arrange for them to need that help before she entered the picture.

She could wish for things to pretty suddenly get dicey in Europe so that the diplomatic Gordons would have to go deal with that but had no way to guarantee it. She might persuade their immediate boss to send them but he wouldn't do so unless there was credible trouble.

There were always personal considerations. It was frustrating that there was no reliable one-pattern-fits-all-cases way to deal with people of some stature. Even when you knew you were so much above them in most, if not all, ways of importance.

Having set things up so she felt certain she could get them shipped away on short notice right at the holiday season, she had to arrange to meet them in person, but in private, and convince them she was sincere and heroically only insisting on her own way for the sake of their peace of mind.

*　*　*

Aunt Sally met the Gordons virtually. That ended up being the best way since it was the only way they would agree to talk to her. And they didn't make up excuses for not doing so in person, simply said they wouldn't do that.

The online meeting didn't last long and didn't go as Dragenlyte intended it to. She was never allowed to make any requests or present any proposals, but did manage to say that this was about the three children and her deep concerns for their welfare.

On to Plan B. At least she had sketched out a plot for what to do if a simple *allow me to do whatever I want with your kids* approach was not enough. Dragenlyte had to convince her government contact to prepare the couple three weeks in advance to be ready for a short-notice several day trip to Eastern Europe at about Christmas Day.

Then he had to trigger that on December 23 when they were at a conference a two-hour drive from the city and wouldn't have time to go home before boarding non-commercial air transport to Europe not quite literally *under the radar*.

Mrs. Norton was taking care of the kids while the Gordons were at the conference and it was the standard arrangement that she would be ready to stay on for a longer period if she got a coded voice message on the apartment's landline phone. The parents sent that message and assume she got it.

For security reasons she could not respond directly to them. Ms. Dragenlyte exploited that weak link in the system.

Accompanied by two unsmiling men in dark suits and ear phones in place, she arrived at the hall door of the apartment after the children were in bed so they didn't see or hear this.

When Mrs. Norton opened the door a bit on the security chain, Dragenlyte waved around a paper she claimed was legal authorization for her to take over here immediately - and requiring Mrs. Norton to gather her things and get out or be arrested.

Mrs. Norton annoyed her by not being terrified or belligerent, only calmly undoing the chain, opening the door, waving them in, then holding out a hand for the document.

Dragenlyte said, "You need special government clearance to even examine this. All you need to know it that I met someone in the business socially and she then on her own checked me out and learned I'm related to the Gordons. She then sought me out and asked me if as a patriotic gesture I would agree to accept responsibility for protecting the kids for as much as several days at any time when they might need to be moved to a safe spot with no delay."

"Even the government isn't so dumb as to issue authorizations or warnings that those who are supposed to be blocked by them are not allowed read and verify," Norton said with a faint smile. "I'm certain that if there were such an authorization, the children's parents would have told me about it to avoid misunderstandings like this."

Dragenlyte insisted, "I signed official papers to be used when and if the parents could not be contacted. They didn't give permission or approval but the papers are on file and go into effect anytime they are sent out of the country. They may not know about that."

Mrs. Norton stepped closer to the men and asked, "Badges?"

They only nodded at Dragenlyte. Ask her any questions.

At that moment there was a light knock on the kitchen door, just loud enough for them to hear.

Norton checked the time and nodded. The two men looked for instructions. Dragenlyte looked like she might either throw up or erupt.

"That's probably the TV reporter and the cameraman who stop by to chat at times. They don't usually stay more than ten minutes."

Mrs. Norton didn't wait for any kind of permission, she headed into the kitchen as the knock was repeated.

When she opened the kitchen door, Mrs. Ormandy - who lived a distance away but was always happy to be paid to spend the night here so the kids would not be alone when Norton went home to attend to things there - waved and stepped in.

Norton hurried to the ajar front door and looked out in time to see the elevator doors close, Dragenlyte and fake agents aboard.

After strongly urging Mrs. Ormandy not to unlock either door no matter what a woman outside said she was required to do, Norton left by the kitchen door and the back door of the building There her ride picked her up and drove her home. She was tempted to ask to be driven slowly by the front of the building to see if the pushy woman was sitting in a parked car deciding what to do next but didn't risk it.

* * *

That September when Sally learned that Toby has been accepted at a respectable local college on a partial scholarship she tried to have an alumnus she could pressure protest that – only to have that person told that to have any import he'd have to be a much bigger donor that he had much prospect of becoming. And the college wouldn't reverse themselves once Toby was accepted and enrolled anyway just because this person wanted to interfere. But they would file a report on the request and their response - and were consulting their legal advisers about whether to inform the targeted student about the matter.

That process had taken three months but ended with the college informing Toby of what had happened. That revelation triggered him to work with his mother to check about the situation with the Gordon parents and, based on feedback from the Gordons, his visit to go check on the Gordon kids today.

Toby wondered and worried if because their parents wouldn't kowtow and agree to be used for her purposes, his Aunt would hope to have their kids misbehave in a public arena where she could claim distress at their shameful and undisciplined behavior and the whispers about that might tarnish the Gordon family name in at least some strata of local society.

His mother and the senior Gordons agreed that they would be distressed but not surprised if something like that was Sally's plan.

Toby then assigned himself the task of trying to keep that from happening. With more than personal vengence involved he would be bold and wary but not intimidated since he knew he was backed by good people as eager as he was to stop such stuff.

For their part, the Gordons were asking for an internal review of exactly who had authorized and apparently micromanaged their recent assignments.

Chapter 10

The center city shopping streets were snowless but festive for the Christmas season with the stores and street fixtures decorated in lights and fake wreaths and greenery. Holiday music played as shoppers hurried along with decorated bags doing the important additional job of advertising their source while keeping the purchases secure.

Several blocks away, the twenty-two stories of apartments in the Whimsicle Condo Building were not the most expensive residences in the city, but they were far from small, inexpensive, or hovels.

Inside, holiday electric candles and other lights decorated many of the windows, including those of the large Gordon family apartment on the Fifteenth floor.

The Gordons' living room was a large, well-furnished space with seasonal decorations all around. At three P.M. on this Christmas Eve the young members of the family were reluctantly gathered here to receive what they feared would be disturbing and unhappy news. Currently twelve year old Marla, nine year old Victor, and and six year old Cindy, sat together on the sofa waiting apprehensively.

Mrs. Osborne had made them breakfast as was usual when she was here overnight and said Mrs. Norton was expected back soon. The three went to their rooms to finish their preps for the day.

A short time later they were summoned to the living room by the voice of Aunt Sally. This was an unexpected turn of events but so far they had no information about what was going on.

Ms. Dragenlyte, elegantly dressed to impress any and all those fortunate enough to view her, stood over them making an only partly successful attempt to look sincerely upset about her news for them.

The presence of Olivia Klemper, their aunt's fifty-plus a bit, oily personal assistant, over at the side of the room smirking with secret amusement since she thought the children couldn't see her or wouldn't understand, reinforced their perception of Aunt Sally as what they had overheard their mother describe to someone as a pretentious schemer. Mom's tone left none of them in doubt about her assessment of Aunt Sally but Marla did have to define the word *pretentious* for Cindy who then got the idea immediately.

Their questions about where Mrs. Osborne or Mrs. Norton were and how these two got in were brushed aside as not things they needed to know, only that until further notice these two women would be in charge. They were at least assured that Mrs. Osborne had rushed off to do some last minute shopping and Mrs. Norton was not sick or dead.

"I know this is disturbing news coming on Christmas Eve, but there's no way I can put off telling you any longer since there are things that need to be done. Through an unfortunate and hard to explain so I won't bother trying mix-up, your parents are off lost somewhere in Eastern Europe and no one is certain when they might return, although of course we hope they will do so eventually. But happily for you, I am in charge of you until they get back and I have some wonderful plans to help you forget them for a while."

"We don't want to forget mommy and daddy," Cindy said, shocked at the very idea of that.

"Especially not on Christmas Eve. No, that's a dumb idea, Aunt Sally," Marla said, shaking her head that this was not okay.

But Ms. Dragenlyte was not interested in their reactions, only in her plans. "There's little point in feeling sad about something you can't change, Marla. And this wonderful apartment that'll be so suitable."

"Suitable for what?" Victor asked, his suspicion evident.

"That's my little surprise, Victor. To take your minds off those who aren't here, I'm throwing a large party here tonight. It'll be ever so much fun I'm sure. Lots of society people who will help our careers."

"I don't have a career. I want mommy and daddy, not society people," Cindy insisted.

An angry look flashed across Dragenlyte's face for a moment, but then she made a show of getting that under control. Warning sent.

Kempler noted that only Cindy seemed impressed by it.

"It surely is always possible that they'll show up alive in a few days or weeks of course, Cindy. But for now I rule," Dragenlyte said in a tone she intended to clearly signal the end of discussion on this topic.

"I can't believe they put you in charge of us. Everybody knows, you don't like kids," Marla said.

Cindy and Victor nodded.

Klemper nodded that it was so and added a shrug.

"What's important is that it's all locked-down legal, Dear. Your parents needed someone to take over in an emergency so, as your mother's cousin, I agreed to the duty and signed the papers. Right now I'm happy that I did. But enough of all, we have a party to prepare for."

"How could you possibly invite these people to a party on such short notice? Or have you been planning this for days without telling us?" Victor asked.

Dragenlyte brushed aside any hint he was correct with a wave of her hand saying, "Of course I must have just found out for certain. Those arrangements hadn't been nailed down yet. Oh, and before I forget, another exciting thing for you to look forward to and prepare your happiest faces for, tomorrow afternoon we'll all have Christmas dinner with some really rich people at their place. I'm sure you'll like that. They have fancy food. Then in the evening I'm having some friends over here for a very nice dinner and you can join us for that if you behave yourselves."

"We always have our Christmas dinner here with mommy and daddy," Cindy said.

"But we're going to expand your horizons and do things a bit different this year. It'll be good for you," Dragenlyte snapped coldly.

"Whose career will that help?" Victor asked sourly, putting the pieces together in his head.

"How can our parents be lost somewhere far away and you act like that's not a problem?" Marla wanted to know.

"Where's Eastern Europe?" Cindy asked of anyone who could give her an answer.

At a cue from her boss, Klemper said loudly, "Enough mit der questions. You vere told what to do, do it! Now!" She gestured for them to react.

Marla shook her head and kept her seat. "I don't think so. You get paid to jump when she says to, but we don't, Ms. Klemper. This isn't our party so we're not gonna have anything to do with it."

Cindy and Victor nodded agreement as all three folded their arms across their chests in a gesture of determination.

"It seems dat der discipline is needed here and I know how to dish that out," Klemper said in a more menacing tone that she would want to have to answer for, while also smiling a bit in anticipation.

"Now, now, Olivia. The children need a few minutes to adjust to the news that changes their plans. We'll let them come around while we arrange things. Do you have the list?"

"How suspiciously convenient," Victor said. "You just learned our apartment's available for you to throw a party tonight, but you already have a to-do list made up."

"I work fast, Victor. I'm know for being highly organized and very determined when I set my mind to something. Remember that and save us both trouble that you'll get the worst part of," Dragenlyte said with a hard edge in her voice now.

"Is that the rest of your claim - that you work fast but sloppy?" Victor asked.

"Should I lock them in der closet vile we work?" Klemper asked without a hint that she might be joking.

Dragenlyte laughed, "You're such a jokester, Olivia. I'm sure they'll be happy to stay out from underfoot and nothing more will need to be done with them."

At that, Marla stood and exited to the kitchen.

Victor and Cindy quickly followed her, casting distrustful looks back at the women.

As she turned to direct the rearrangement of the large room Dragenlyte lamented sarcastically, "Oh dear, I fear they don't love me above all others. Oh well, at least they'll be useful."

"Unless you push too much. They start to whine so the party guests hear and the hosts who hired you get upset and ask vhat is doing and did they make der big mistook mit you."

"I'll depend on you to deal with the three of them firmly in such a case so I can say I don't know what has come over them or you, but clearly they came to ruin the evening with nasty little lies," Dragenlyte said with a dismissive wave.

After a long pause, she could still see that Klemper was tapping a foot and waiting for something, but she didn't know what.

When she gestured for an explanation, Klemper said, "I do not have you trained good yet. Could this be ein trouble? I am vhaiting to hear more."

Then Dragenlyte got it. "of course you will get a nice bonus for taking care of any awkward moments with the children. Didn't I say that? I think of it as so automatic that I don't need to say it every time."

"Und I am still training you to alvays say it to reassure me since I see many things and know when you say you will do a thing but never intend for to do it or actually do it," Klemper said. "I vorry den. It vould be awkward to tell all I could tell."

"Of course you'll be well taken care of. Now focus on the party."

"Dat is vhat I am doing."

"I don't know why you worry so much."

"My memory is better than yours at some of the times. Dat you should not forget," Klemper said with a hint of challenge in her tone.

Chapter 11

Dragenlyte and Klemper entered the large, nicely decorated master bedroom of the Gordon condo, checked that the children were not in sight so they might come eavesdropping, and closed the door.

Dragenlyte then said, "So the party tonight should put me in with half a dozen couples whose names I can drop in the proper circles and get more cachet."

"Plus you surely will be well paid for arranging the party for the Harbisons who are der actual hosts but didn't decide to do a party until the usual places were all booked," Klemper noted. She was usually willing to go along but not willing to ignore the facts.

"Plus, they wanted a homey environment but can't be bothered messing up their own place with a party. Rest assured, you'll get your bonus, Olivia, you don't need to remind me of that as a subtle hint at blackmail."

"It always helps to know vhat certain people aren't supposed to find out."

"Then tomorrow I'll get points for providing the children as props at the Charleston's dinner. They'll be grandchildren for a wealthy couple who never had children – but little stand-ins who will nicely disappear after an hour or two before the old couple get tired of them."

"You cover all der bases," Klemper conceded.

"As long as it's to my advantage."

"What about Mr. Austin Noble? Is it prudent to try to fool him?"

"I'm not trying to fool him, I just want a chance to have him see another side of me since I suspect he cares about that," Dragenlyte replied a bit defensively.

"You've changed der plan? You vil not say dey are yours?"

"No, no. That was only a passing thought. I realized I couldn't keep that up even if I arranged to keep their parents out of the picture on secret diplomatic missions for a year. Those kids won't play along no matter what I offer them. No, they're my young charges and I'm fondly nurturing them, but only during a family emergency."

"Dat makes more sense. I didn't see you pulling off the other plan."

"The revised plan still means I need to make it look good when he's here but I'm a good enough actress for that. The problem will be to keep the little monsters from acting out. He has to see them up close, not in photos or videos, but the less they say to him or him to them, the better for me. It's much easier to fake what you want to have said than to have to explain away what you didn't want to deal with"

"A firm hand is vhat they need. They must know there vill be big unpleasantness if they cause a disturbance. But no bruises that show."

"I want to believe you're joking, Olivia, but I don't want to know about it if you need to do such things. You'd better go see what they're doing so they don't slow things up."

* * *

From junior high on, Sally took the position that since money is power she should always ally herself in whatever ways possible or called for with moneyed people. Her goal was to use their power second hand while she amassed enough to have power of her own.

To convince herself she didn't need to have sex with them to join the rich people, she focused on rich and powerful businesswoman Andrea "Doria" Charmerhaha - who started her own ascent by marrying money. Thus Sally would show, without being overt about it until she wrote her autobiography as the frosting on her career in her old age (as she expected to do, so she was collecting memories in a series of paper diaries kept under lock and key - with another copy of everything in supposedly totally safe password locked files on a laptop.

In those texts she openly admitted that she knew from the start that she was better than the Andrea Doria in everything from the start and had simply used her as a convenient tool. By the time she was ready to publish, the old woman would be gone and with her most of those witnesses who might contradict that and present examples to float arguments about which used the other more often and effectively.

She got a thrill from recording diary notes as soon as possible after deciding on some plan to get noticed or more. Not one who could remember a secret code system for text, she often brought the laptop to events where she would try to keep it out of sight of anyone else but slip to it and make notes on juicy bits for that biography - or maybe a lightly shrouded novel if she saw things that made others look bad and decided to take that tangent to fame and fortune.

Only when Klemper was gone did she get the laptop out of the dresser drawer where she had hidden it when she first arrived. It was time to make notes on how she had dealt with the children and she wanted to remember her firm words to them.

Dragenlyte got that the Gordon kids' fights against Klemper were really against her and resented that. Especially that Klemper laughed at her for expecting her to always control the kids when she expected and needed her to but without expecting much in return.

* * *

Klemper smiled and began to move items in the living room.

Marla waved to Victor - who ran at Klemper as if to grab her but stopped short and out of her reach to check what she was touching.

With that apparent attempt at a distraction, Marla put a lego block basket she had made and put silk flowers into inside a fancy square scarf and tied that at the top like a Hershey's kiss.

She made sure to glance around twice as if thinking that she was hiding a candy stash from Klemper.

As soon as Marla stepped away from that, Klemper clomped over and "accidentally" threw it hard onto the floor to be sure it broke.

"Oopsie. Too bad for dat."

She expected tears and protests. Cindy was certainly on the brink of those. Marla and Victor were dry-eyed but resigned. They also resisted any hints of satisfaction or glee.

Marla untied the scarf and with a minimum of moves made sure the basket was close to completely disassembled and the silk flowers were tattered and torn. She carried the scarf and its contents to the bedroom door, then held it on top of both hands..

She called, "Aunt Sally, your servant broke my craft shop flower basket that you wanted to show to the guests."

That brought Dragenlyte to the door in a flash to see what was the matter. It also prompted Klemper to mutter to her self.

Marla tossed the loose pile of plastic pieces at Dragenlyte who automatically tried to grab them, but at the odd feel of the loose jumble let it fall to the floor where lego blocks scattered about.

Dragenlyte glared at Klemper - and got that right back.

"I'm sure you can put it back together, dear. After all, It wasn't a difficult project," Aunt Sally said.

"Why bother since she'll find an excuse to break it again."

"Enough mit dis nonsense, fix it and be done mit this."

Marla turned and walked to the far side of the room and sat down. Cindy was close behind her.

Victor edging toward another area of the room as obviously sneaky as he could be without being blatantly so.

"She broke it, so make her fix it," Marla called.

Dragenlyte looked at the debris on the floor as she considered doing exactly that.

"But don't expect me to not tell what happened to it to anyone who asks. Not at any party ever," Marla said.

Dragenlyte tried to focus her disappointment on Marla - who was having none of it - while she meant it for Klemper - who got that but was having none if it either.

"Too bad. So sad. The fine people visiting here today will go away knowing the Gordon children can't do anything they or their parents are proud of. Too bad, but that's how it is," Dragenlyte said.

"And we don't have an aunt who can figure out how to put lego blocks together either. Will that surprise them?" Marla asked.

That raised the hackles of both women.

And triggered Victor, the practiced distractor. He rushed over and grabbed an eight-inch-tall dark-colored plastic bottle shaped like a gorilla from a head-high book shelf and turned his back to the women to protect it.

"You leave this alone. This is my special thing from our exciting trip last year."

He tried not to let it be seen but couldn't actually hide it as he pulled books on the next lower shelf as if to put the bottle behind them.

Then he stepped away with his hands held crossed at his chest as if holding it.

With a derisive snort, Klemper stomped over to get that from behind the books - as he backed away from her but into a corner.

There he turned to face the wall to do something unseen.

There was no gorilla behind the books.

Determined now, Klemper grabbed him - and he squeezed the now uncapped flexible plastic gorilla filled with dark colored water to look more realistic into her face and down the front of her as she gasped and stepped back in surprise.

Then he ran to the kitchen with the bottle to wash off his hands, the only part of him that got wet.

As Klemper stood getting over her shock and assessing how messy she looked, Dragenlyte laughed out loud at the unexpected turn of events. Then she caught herself and was furious with Victor and all the Gordons - and embarrassed by her first reaction.

"How are you going to explain this away?" Marla said, more to herself than to her Aunt. Cindy sat terrified.

"Quickly, quickly. Go get showered off and rinse out your clothes. Fortunately I insisted you bring a change just in case. There's a dryer. If that didn't stain... Go and get cleaned up. The hired people could be here any minute and I don't want questions."

"You need to think about who can reveal the most if der are questions you could have bought off. This is the rough, real world," Klemper said quietly but to be sure she was heard.

* * *

Later, who can say why Marla placed a simple rubber duck into a colored bag and walked across the living room holding the bag first at her back, then at her side, so Klemper - in her second and less attractive set of clothes - saw the action but not what the girl was hiding.

Marla walked on, and as she passed Victor standing surveying the room, she handed off the bag to him.

He is turn handed it off to Cindy sitting calmly on the sofa - but without the bag. Cindy smiled at having a favorite toy to hold.

But Klemper started for that spot to find out what the secret item was and confiscate it and once on the move she couldn't seem to rein herself in. Klemper grabbed the rubber duck.

Cindy cried in anger and fear. Marla, Victor, and Dragenlyte stared at her stealing a child's simple toy.

"Enough mit der nonsense. Get into Wictor's bedroom to be out of der vay and to decide vhat you must wear to look presentable, not slouching like not at an important party. Now. Or I vhip your bottoms hard."

"Are you the person actually in charge here as you say or not, Miss Dragenlyte?" Marla called. "Are you accepting responsibility and the consequences of your hired help threatening us in our home?"

"She's only exaggerating for effect because you three are being brats. As long as you do exactly what you're told when you're told there will be no need to spank anyone," Dragenlyte said.

"We'll be sure to quote you about much of what you've said here tody. Imagine the stories we'll have to retell by tomorrow night," Marla said.

"Who will believe children against an adult?" Dragenlyte said.

"When the adult has a reputation like yours according to my parents, most people," Marla said and walked away.

"Dat is not a happy thought, but she has it right," Klemper said.

The three kids walked calmly into the kitchen together and for the moment neither woman moved to force them anywhere else.

Chapter 12

Inside, the three young Gordons reacted with surprise to a light knock on the kitchen door to the outside hallway.

Marla went to that door and called quietly, "Who's there?"

The response was also quietly delivered. "Cousin Toby Jansen. Is it safe for me to come in? Is the Dragon Lady there?"

Marla opened the door and admitted nineteen-year-old who looked cautiously around the room before he stepped in and closed the door. He was dressed to not be noticed - topped with a balaclava ski mask he could pull down to not be identified if he decided the situation called for that.

"Aunt Sally's in the living room. Do you want to talk to her?" Marla asked.

Toby whispered, "No. At least for now I don't want her to know I'm around. What did she tell you about your folks?"

Cindy whispered, "They're lost in a place called Eastern Europe."

"But Aunt Sally's throwing parties tonight and tomorrow like it doesn't matter," the unhappy Victor pointed out.

Toby gestured that they should speak quietly. "I was afraid it was something like this. First, I can assure you that your parents are fine, but because of their job can't get home tonight as they had hoped."

"Is Aunt Sally only doing this so she can use our apartment to throw parties she hopes will impress people?" Marla asked. "Mom says she always seem to do things hoping to impress people."

Toby nodded that the girl was correct. "But there's more to it than that this time. Someone has started a rumor that she's out to bag a husband and I suspect you kids are critical to her plan."

"She wants to marry us?" Cindy found that idea confusing.

"No, she wants to use you kids as bait to impress the man she has her eye on," Toby said.

"She wants to look maternal?" Marla asked, getting the idea but having trouble with the image with her aunt in it.

"I think that's the idea," Toby replied. "She's a user and ruining your holidays is of no concern to her. But she could too easily make it even worse."

"What could be worse than spending Christmas with her and the snooty people she wants to fool?" Victor asked.

"From something I heard, she has some influence with someone in high places and she actually arranged for your parents to be sent on this special diplomatic mission to keep them away for Christmas."

"That dirty rat!" Victor grumbled.

Toby gestured that there was more to consider. "The scarier idea is that if she thinks it'll help her plans, she might be able to get your parents assigned to jobs that'll keep them away from home for weeks."

"Why would she do that?" sweet, innocent Cindy asked.

"So she can impress some man that she's the motherly type and taking care of her young relatives for more than one night," Marla said.

"That's what I'm afraid of," Toby agreed. "I've had my problems with her over the years and I came here today to see if I can keep you from the same fate."

"We're ready to be saved from her," Victor replied.

The three young Gordons were talking quietly when Klemper entered and saw Toby. With no hesitation, she ordered, "You! You are not velcome here. Out!"

Marla said quietly but firmly, "He's my guest. And I live here, I'm not just a hired help day visitor."

"Your aunt is in charge while your parents are far away and I am her deputy so what I say goes."

"Right out the window where it belongs," Victor said, enjoying that opening to talk back without being too obvious.

"Don't defy me or you vil regret it," Klemper warned.

Always sweet and innocent, Cindy asked, "Do you know why it changed? Why was nice Mrs. Norton taking care of us until today and suddenly Aunt Dragon Lady says it's her job?"

Klemper gestured for the girl to keep her voice down. "Don't you dare let her hear you call her that name. That's the no-no big."

"But what's the answer to the question?" Marla asked. "Or do we have to call Mr. Eustace the lawyer and ask?"

"You vill get no answer and ask no questions, only do as you are told. Children must know their place," Klemper said with a small snort.

She was not about to defend or even explain how as part of her preps for this day, Dragenlyte had hired someone to snoop and report back on the routines and helpers here. Then paid someone to gather somewhat detailed info on Mrs. Norton, the most usual day sitter, and Mrs. Ormandy, the occasional overnight sitter.

It was a lot of trouble but this was an important day planned weeks in advance so her preps were elaborate. When she had to leave the night before since she sensed that the hired men would not touch Mrs. Norton, Dragenlyte made a call from a street pay phone.

That set in motion a two-step small subterfuge arranged on an *If needed* basis two weeks earlier.

About six A.M. a man snuck to a house a two hour drive from the city and cut the phone line. He made a few dollars days before for checking that the elderly man resident didn't have cell phone access.

Then he made a pay phone call from that town to Mrs. Norton.

He left a message on her landline phone machine saying she should check on her father since he wasn't answering his phone. He ended before she picked up so she could not ask for more details.

As Dragenlyte had hoped, Mrs. Norton called Mrs. Ormandy and asked if she could stay a few extra hours while she drove out to check on her father. Agreed.

Dragenlyte barged in after Ormandy opened the front door to see what was happening when there was a knock but she couldn't see anyone in the hall when she peeked out with the security chain on.

A wave of an official looking document and assurance that the bearer had government-backed authority to take over and protect the children. Ormandy hesitated - then an handful of cash to run and buy gifts that she hadn't been able to until now in return for not telling anyone what was happening - in the interest of national defense.

Ormandy was gone, Dragenlyte and Klemper owned the place. All of that accomplished before the kids came out looking for breakfast.

And here they were now an hour later, fed but not happy.

"It also helps if they know their rights," Victor said.

Klemper said to Toby, "This must be more of your doing. You are churning up the problems as usual."

"I can't claim credit for these guys not being easily intimidated or fooled. I'd say their parents are doing a great job with them though. I applaud and support their determination to defend themselves," he replied with a smile.

"I will call for the police to remove you if you are not gone right now!" Klemper said to end this situation.

"Good, then we can ask the police to check on why Mrs. Norton isn't here as she was supposed to be," Marla said with a deliberate show of enthusiasm for the idea. "They won't sidestep the question and probably won't let you do so either. Let me go call them in case you can't figure out the number. We know you get things turned around and think yes means no and stuff like that."

Marla walked out, heading for the phone in the next room with Cindy right behind her. Victor stayed here looking defiantly at Klemper.

"You, out. Go with your sisters."

"No, I'll stay here so I can report on anything you say to cousin Toby since I don't trust your honesty, Ms. Olive Oil."

"My name is Olivia - but to you it is always Ms. Klemper, brat!"

"Meanwhile the police are being called," Toby reminded her.

Klemper hesitated, debating with herself about what to do, then turned and hurried out muttering, "Yes, she maybe vil do it and that vil not be helpful."

Victor gave Toby a thumbs-up and followed Klemper out.

* * *

As Klemper entered the living room where Marla stood by the phone, there was a knock at the front door.

Cindy pushed a chair over to block Klemper's path long enough for Marla to get to the door first and open it a bit.

The caterer, Mr. Pierre, and several liveried workers were there with boxes of catering equipment. Mr. Pierre stepped forward but was forced to stop short since Marla didn't fully open the door. "It's Mr. Pierre the caterer, Honey. Tell mommy we've arrived."

"Mommy isn't here and she didn't hire anyone, thank you."

Klemper ran over and grabbed the door to open it, trying to shove Marla aside in the process but the girl stood firm.

Cindy followed the woman over.

When Klemper pinched Marla to make her move, Cindy kicked Klemper hard in the shin. "Out of the way. Ow, oh!"

Mr. Pierre put a hand on the door to push it open but hesitated for a moment when Marla said, "One step inside and you're invading our home and I start shouting."

"Don't play games, little girl." He pushed the door open and stepped inside.

Marla shouted loudly, "Help! Help! Get out of here!"

Klemper raised her hand as if to slap Marla which prompted Cindy to shout, "Stop hurting us."

Then she screamed - loud, long, shrill, and terror-filled.

Mr. Pierre scowled at this nonsense. However, when one of his workers tapped his arm, he turned and looked down the hall - where two neighbors stood at their open doors watching with concern now, one conspicuously with a cell phone in hand.

Dragenlyte came out of the bedroom to find Klemper limping after Cindy who was running for safety behind Victor - who wielded a baseball bat and an expression saying he'd use it and likely even enjoy the excuse.

Then she saw Mr. Pierre facing Marla and looking disgusted outside the open front door. She called, "What's the problem, Pierre? Get in here. There's no time to waste."

"I've been denied admittance."

"By whom?" Dragenlyte asked, confused.

"By me," Marla said. She added quietly to Dragenlyte, "Want to test if the neighbors will call the police and maybe come to our rescue with their guns if I keep shouting that these people aren't allowed in no matter what a piece of paper you claim to have says?"

Mr. Pierre was looking down the hall with some concern.

Dragenlyte stalked forward in full intimidation mode to stare at the girl close-up, flexing her hands as if preparing to grab and muffle

Marla – and only then noticed the large sharp scissors Marla had taken from her pocket and clutched.

Dragenlyte took a small step back and said, "I'm sorry, Pierre, there's obviously been a misunderstanding. Give me just a minute to straighten things out."

Mr. Pierre nodded stiffly and turned, nose high in the air, to fuss over non-existent problems with a worker's uniform.

Dragenlyte forced a smile as she pushed the door closed, then turned, fury in her eye, to confront the three children who had now regrouped by the door. "Let's get a few things clear so I don't have to take firm actions we'd all prefer not to think about."

Toby approached from where he had watched all this from the kitchen doorway. Klemper moved into position and prepared to tackle him if that seemed called for.

Dragenlyte was surprised to see Toby here but expected him to be here to fight with her about what she had recently done to cause him trouble just as on-going harassment. Or to accuse her of cheating and cutting corners in a variety of situations in which she was a minor player. At another time she might get satisfaction from a verbal duel with him, but today she had important things to do.

Oh yes, that included dealing with a trio of brats who were important to her detailed plans but had decided to act up. And Mr. Pierre was left standing out in the hall. The stories he might spread about her control of things - or lack thereof.

Toby said pleasantly, "May I suggest a solution? Why don't the kids go for a drive out to the country with me and leave the place for you to fix up?"

"Mind the business of yourself," Klemper grumbled.

"A drive in the country would be fun," Marla said.

Dragenlyte pondered, probably not intending to say it out loud, "What would it take to persuade them to go along? No, wait. What did she say?"

"It's gonna bother us a lot to watch you change our home all around to please your hoity-toity guests, so we'd rather not have to watch it," Victor said, sensing what his sister and cousin had in mind.

"But you'll be back in time for the party," Dragenlyte said.

"That's the idea. *Weather permitting* of course," Toby agreed.

"I say do not be trusting them. Never give the opposition what they want," Klemper warned.

Dragenlyte said breezily, "I'm glad I thought of that. It's agreed. Toby will take the three youngsters for a drive while I supervise the party preparations."

Feeling at his pockets, Toby said, "Oh wait, I don't have enough money for gas. I can't do that after all."

Dragenlyte snapped, "Olivia, give him some of that cash I gave you to tip the caterer's people who give us useful feedback on who's saying what."

Without waiting for any other developments she opened the front door and called, "Pierre, come in and get set up."

Klemper muttered under her breath as she forked over some cash. To her further annoyance, Toby reached and took many more bills than the older woman intended from her hand.

Dragenlyte waved imperiously for Klemper to show the caterers where to set up and not dispute the money.

Klemper resolved to replenish that cash from the handbag in the bedroom as a priority. But first things first.

Chapter 13

As Toby entered the master bedroom, Marla stood watch by the phone, Cindy and Victor by the hall to the bedrooms.

In the master bedroom, Toby took out a notebook and dialed a number on the bedside phone, keeping an eye on the closed door.

"Hi, I'm calling about renting a house."

A moment later Toby smiled as he made a note in his book. "Yes, I'm delighted that it's available too. I'm looking forward to seeing it and spending two nights there. Let me verify a few details with you."

*　*　*

While the caterers bustled between from dining room and kitchen, Dragenlyte came out of the kitchen and noticed the children in those spots and became suspicious.

She ambled toward Marla who stepped over to a decorative pile of wrapped packages, her expression suggesting guilt and worry as she adjusted the boxes as if hiding something among them.

This had the intended effect of distracting Dragenlyte from the phone where the indicator light showed that a call was being made.

Marla moved to another spot and again acted overly innocent.

Dragenlyte acted as if she were simply adjusting the same group of boxes while she looked for whatever contraband might be hidden there - but found nothing.

Dragenlyte acted nonchalant as she looked around the room.

Victor sneaked over - knowing she was watching him out of the corner of her eye - and casually moved a drape to look out the window. Then he adjusted the drape as if might be hiding something before he moved away.

Dragenlyte took the long way to that spot and adjusted the same drape now that Victor had moved. She found nothing suspicious, incriminating, or that warranted further attention.

When Dragenlyte seemed to focus on the hall to the bedrooms Cindy ran to the front door, opened it and looked outside, then closed it and pressed her back to it as if to keep anyone else from looking out there.

As Dragenlyte considered that, Toby came from the bedroom area, making it clear he had been washing his hands.

"I wondered where you were," Dragenlyte said, then went back into the kitchen as Klemper came out of there.

Toby winked at the kids who relaxed and gathered at the sofa.

Klemper began to gather the framed family photos and other personal items from around the room.

Marla shouted, "Leave our pictures alone. You have no right to touch those things. They belong in here."

Klemper ignored her and continued her task. She carried the first group of items over and put them in a cabinet.

Toby sat to watch what would happen now. The kids were on their own, but his experience with them was that they were resourceful.

Victor positioned himself to block Klemper's access to one group of items so she simply picked up others.

Marla and Cindy took the first items placed in the cabinet and, as Klemper put her second batch of items in there, they returned family things to their original positions.

Klemper noted the items missing from the cabinet and spotted them when she turned back to the room.

"Okay, I teach a lesson called the power of the key," Klemper said as she locked the cabinet with a key in the door and took the key with her as she made a circuit to pick up the first items again. When the girls saw they now couldn't get at the second batch of items they let their frustration show.

Klemper locked the second batch of items in the cabinet with a great smirk of triumph.

The kids huddled and had a whispered conference as Klemper leisurely gathered other personal items from around the room and locked them away in that cabinet.

Victor walked nonchalantly to the kitchen.

As Klemper moved to remove several framed drawings done by the children, the girls moved to block her. "These are ours. We made them and they're supposed to stay here," Cindy insisted.

Klemper snorted, "Nobody but the mommy and the daddy think they're nice and mommy and daddy are not here so neither will these be during the parties." She leaned closer and added, "But if I have any trouble about them, oops they get broken and torn to pieces and isn't that too bad."

"You're not a nice person," Cindy told her angrily.

"I don't get paid to be nice, only to do what I am told."

* * *

As the caterers moved around in the kitchen, Victor went to a cabinet drawer and searched through its contents.

He smiled when he found what he was looking for and carefully pocketed a ring of keys, careful not to let anyone else see what that was.

Dragenlyte turned from conferring with Mr. Pierre to watch Victor leave. The boy forced himself to be blank-faced.

* * *

Victor joined his sister in the living room and after a whispered conference the three went to Toby.

Marla said, "Ms. Olive Oily reminded us that there are keys to the bedroom and even the bathroom doors. We have them and think we should use them. What do you think, Toby?"

"You want to lock everything up and hide the keys before you go? I love the idea as long as I don't have to be around to hear Aunt Sally scream when she finds out."

"Although that might be fun," Victor noted.

* * *

Ten minutes later Dragenlyte watched from the kitchen door as Toby checked that each child had a coat and a backpack. At a nod from Toby that they were ready to go, Dragenlyte nodded back her approval.

The foursome were half out the door when Klemper hurried in from the bedroom hallway shouting, "Stop, vandals! Dis you cannot do."

"What's the problem, Olivia?" Dragenlyte asked, eager to be rid of the small distractions.

Marla said, "We want to thank your not very nice assistant. We learned a useful lesson from her."

"A lesson?" Dragenlyte didn't understand the reference but she was instantly suspicious of anything the kids approved of.

"It's called the power of the key. You'll figure it out before too long," Victor said with a big smile.

"Do not let them go! Search the bags," Klemper demanded.

"Happy holidays to all," Toby called as he shooed the children ahead of him and closed the door behind them.

Dragenlyte tried to keep Klemper from chasing after them since she didn't understand what her assistant was protesting but feared the woman had gone over the edge and might create new problems by attacking them with the catering people here.

Klemper insisted, "They have locked the doors! We need the keys."

"Locked what doors?" Dragenlyte asked, confused.

"To the bedrooms. And the bathrooms."

Dragenlyte had her doubts about this as she hurried to check the bedrooms. Klemper waited for a reaction.

"They'll pay for this!" Dragenlyte shouted when she confirmed the report.

Klemper shrugged. She had done what she could. "But you must pay right now. We vill never find der keys. We must call the locksmith before he goes home for his Christmas."

Dragenlyte stomped back into the room and demanded, "What did the brat mean that you taught them what to do?"

"Do not be going there. No good will come of it when you are in need of my fully cooperating."

Dragenlyte wanted to demand answers and vent some fury but she recognized that she might lose a lot if she lost this woman's help.

Chapter 14

As Toby drove them along a rural road in the late afternoon the three Gordon children gawked at the unfamiliar scenery.

"I've never seen the country like this before," Cindy said.

"We've been on vacations but those were trips to the airport and resorts at the other end of the flights. I think I was in the real country like this once or twice when I was a kid," Marla commented.

Toby cleared his throat and announced, "It's first decision time, Guys. I wanted to get you away from Aunt Sally for a while before I said anything about this. I've made plans so you can stay away if you want. I've rented a house for tonight and tomorrow night so you can escape being pawns in the Dragon Lady's schemes - but only if you want to."

"But you told her we'd be back," Victor said, a note of worry about being involved in a lie tainting his tone.

"I said *weather permitting*," Toby clarified.

"That's exactly what you told her," Victor said, liking this idea.

"There's a significant snowstorm on its way so if we agreed it was best not to drive in that, I wouldn't have lied."

"Won't she drive out and get us?" Marla asked. "She really hates having her plans not work out."

"An important part of my plan is that she doesn't know where we are and we won't let her know," Toby answered. "We'll assure her that we're safe but that's all."

"How will you do that?"

"Leave the details to me, Victor. I know a way," Toby said.

"Will Santa Claus know where we are?" Cindy asked in a wee voice, half afraid of the answer.

"Of course," Marla assured her. "He may leave our presents for us at home but we'll get them."

"What's the house you rented like?" Victor asked.

"We'll all see soon. Here's a sign for the town of Festivity, our destination," Toby said.

*   *   *

The sun was low in the sky when the four scrambled out of the car outside the Quade house, a large old country house with a roofed porch on the front, an arbor up the side, and a large central chimney.

"It belongs to a man named Mr. Quade but he doesn't live in it himself anymore," Toby explained. "My mom heard rumors of Aunt Sally coming here and having some kind of a fuss with Mr. Quade back about the time I was born. When I told her what I wanted to do to keep Sally from using you guys, Mom told me who to call here in town to check if the house could be rented. It could and here we are."

"It's like a house in a picture," Cindy said loving it at first view.

"It'll look extra nice if it snows," Marla commented.

"There'll be at least enough of a threat of that to keep us here until Christmas is over if you want to," Toby said.

"There's someone in there! I saw a movement at the window," Cindy shouted, not sure if that was a problem.

"That'll be Mrs. Lapinski. She came over to turn the heat up and make sure it was ready for us," Toby said.

Mrs. Lapinski came out the front door and waved.

"Should we take our bags in with us now?" Victor asked.

"Sure. And thanks for being smart enough to not ask a lot of questions at first. Congratulations too on keeping it simple so you could fit clothes for two days in your backpacks without arousing the Dragon Lady's suspicions."

"She doesn't know our routines so when I said we always take backpacks with us everywhere, she didn't argue," Marla noted. "I guess that's the maternal touch where she's concerned."

Toby and Marla chuckled at that. Victor wasn't sure he got the hidden meaning. Cindy didn't care, she was too busy enjoying the view of the house.

Backpacks in hand, they headed into the house.

* * *

The living room of the Quade house was a large room with a front window to the porch, a side window, and a large fireplace at the back facing the porch. There was a wide doorway to the dining room on each side of that. There was comfortable furniture scattered around.

There were no holiday decorations in sight.

Toby and the three Gordons stood with Mrs. Lapinski out in the entryway at the bottom of the stairs to the second floor.

Mrs. Lapinski said, "Fred Quade moved out a few years back. He has another house in town. The strange things made him nervous."

"What strange things?" Cindy asked, interested and prepared to be worried.

"Nothing for you to worry about I'm pretty sure. I don't believe it's really cursed, but funny things do happen here. I don't know if the birds or the sweep spooked Fred the most."

"Something happened with birds? Inside?" Victor asked.

"Oh, Fred spilled a bag of small seeds on the floor in here and went to get a broom to clean up from his car. A neighbor says she saw a whole flock of birds sucked right down the chimney as they flew over. Anyway they ate up all the seeds and when Fred came back in through the front door they flew out that way scaring him pretty bad."

The Gordons exchanged looks of amused wonder at that.

"He must have thought that those birds were attacking him or something," Toby said to make it all seem less spooky.

"But what's a sweep?" Cindy asked, still a bit leery.

"Oh, I meant a chimney sweep. A fellow who cleans the soot out of the chimney. The local fellow won't do this house anymore. Strange what he says happened to him."

"Did he find something dead in there? Victor asked.

"No, he says the chimney spat him out."

What does that mean?" Marla asked.

"He swears he looked down the chimney from the roof to see if there were any obvious problems and he was sucked right down into the fireplace over there. Then before he could fully recover his senses, he shot back up the chimney and landed on his back on the roof."

"Or maybe he bumped his head and knocked himself out and imagined it," Toby suggested to sound confident.

"Maybe so, but he swears that he was clean when he started but covered with soot when he picked himself up on the roof. As far as I know though no one's ever been harmed in here, just sort of mystified."

"It sounds like an interesting place," Victor decided.

"A good way to put it, Lad. Since no one has been living here there are no decorations up but there are some around if you want to put them up," Mrs. Lapinski noted.

The woman looked out the window as Rudolf Rambler drove his pickup truck by and slowed to check out the house that was usually dark. "That's Rudolf. He's planning to open his present to himself tonight and spoil his Christmas surprise."

"Rudolf the reindeer?" Cindy asked in wonder.

"Oh, no. Rudolf Rambler's his name. He's a nice man but doesn't understand about the fun of surprises."

"But if he bought a gift for himself, wouldn't he know what it is anyway?" Victor asked.

"But he could still act surprised," Mrs. Lapinski replied.

Toby and the Gordons exchanged *Is she kidding?* looks.

Mrs. Lapinski pointed to the stairs and gestures to the upper level as she said, "There are three bedrooms but only the one bath. The back room has three single beds, the others each have one full size. I put out linens but you'll have to make up the beds. Fred rents the place out now and then which is why you're here so he keeps the basics stocked. There are plenty of blankets."

Marla ran her finger tips up a wall. "This is wallpaper isn't it? I don't think I've ever seen any before."

"We have oyster shell colored paint on our walls so they can be washed clean," Cindy explained to the woman.

"This is an old house and the decor is old fashioned too by some tastes but it works nice in here," Mrs. Lapinski said.

None of her small audience disagreed.

"I want the room nearest the stairs!" Victor shouted to establish his first dibs claim.

"I'm sure we'll be comfortable here, Mrs. Lapinski," Toby said.

Next, they all walked into the large dining room. The space was dominated by the large table in the center with eight matching chairs. The door to the kitchen was open at one end.

Mrs. Lapinski said, "There's this big table to eat at. The kitchen's ready for use. There are plates and glasses and all. And lots of pots and pans. But there's no food in the fridge. You have to fix your own meals, a cook doesn't come with the house."

"We'll be fine in that department," Toby said. "Thank you for your help in settling us in, Mrs. Lapinski. I have your number in case we have any real problems. It's very important that I talk to Mr. Quade about paying for our stay. I hope he got the word on that but please remind him when you give him a report on us as we expect.

As Mrs. Lapinski nodded and left, Toby and the Gordons took seats at the table.

"This is a big table. I like it," Cindy said running her hands over the polished wood.

"It's so big you might get lost walking around it," Victor joked.

"Later we'll take another vote on staying in case anyone wants to change his or her mind. We're playing this by ear so anything can be changed," Toby informed them.

"Why would we change our minds?" Victor asked.

"Because some things you might rightly expect as part of your Christmas celebration aren't likely if we stay here," Toby said. He was determined to be realistic about this adventure.

"Like what?" Cindy asked.

"Like presents and a decorated tree and a big breakfast and a turkey dinner and carols playing and television and fancy wrapping paper," Marla blurted out.

Then she stopped, aware that she may have revealed that she has been thinking about such things more than she wanted to admit.

"We won't have any of that?" Cindy asked, seriously considering that possibility for the first time.

"Rather, we won't have some parts of it the way you're used to," Toby said. "I don't see how you'll have some of it until you go home. So we choose between the familiar kind and a different kind of festivity."

"In the little town of Festivity," Victor noted.

"We won't get any presents at all?" Cindy asked with a small plaintive note in her voice.

"We'll see what we can find to buy for one another here in town using some more of Aunt Sally's money that Ms. Klemper so happily handed over for our use if we had any problems. Being hungry is a problem, Buy ourselves food solves it," Toby told her. "She doesn't know it yet, but I used her name and arranged to trade a debt owed to her by the owner for the rent on this house so we're her guests. At least a few people she interacted with years ago still live here."

That was interesting news to the others.

"Friends of hers?" Marla asked with a note of concern.

"From what I could find out she probably doesn't have a friend in the whole town after what she was involved in," Toby said.

"Remember, the gifts we'd have gotten tomorrow will still be waiting at home for us if we decide to wait an extra day to get them," Victor said. His vote was firmly in the *Stay* column.

"And remember that going back for those presents tomorrow means going back to Aunt Sally and her plans to use us," Marla pointed out to Cindy. Marla was a *Stay* vote too.

They all looked at Cindy who wasn't sure yet. She had a lot of new things to consider.

"But we'll decide about that later," Toby suggested.

"We don't have to head back right away if we decide that would be the better thing to do. We're making this up as we go along and can change our minds as long as we all agree to the changes," Toby said.

Chapter 15

It was early evening when Toby, coat on, stood alone out on the porch making a cell phone call. "Shane, it's Toby Jansen. Hello and Merry Christmas to you, buddy."

"Hey, Toby, what do you need my help with this time? Oh, and same to you about the merry thing."

"I'm tempted to claim to be hurt that you think I only call when I need your help, but I do in a big way right now so I'm soft-pedaling that. You know my Aunt Sally right?"

"Ms. Dragenlyte, a.k.a. the Dragon Lady? I know her and I'm scared of her. I think I should hang up now. I'm not going anywhere near that one."

"I only want you to call and relay a message to her. My young cousins are depending on you."

"Go ahead, use little kids to manipulate my heart strings."

"Shane, buddy, you're the perfect person to do this since you're so good at playing dumb."

"Compliments shouldn't make the difference and I don't think that was one anyway."

"What I meant is that you can do this and not let her know who you are while convincing her you're so out of it that there's no point in pursuing you."

"I don't want her pursuing me!"

"So she won't be able to. Won't even think about it."

"Let me try this from the other side. What's in this for me other than the thrill of living dangerously?"

Toby smiled. He was ready if it came to this.

"Sweet revenge and the complete Gilbert and Sullivan operetta CD collection," Toby said.

" Ooh, I like the sound of sweet revenge but it's better if I have an actual comeuppance to savor. Do I have one?"

"Who do you think nixed you getting that job because of your haircut? That was the Dragon Lady. The manager wanted her to put in a good word with someone and you were a token of his willingness to follow orders when she wanted payback."

"I didn't know that. I thought the hair thing was his own warped idea. And since then I've learned enough about him and his business to be glad to not be mixed up in it. But wait, she wasn't around that day."

"She made a phone call, which is all that I'm asking you to do in return. Just tell her her charges are safe, not to worry."

"If it's a message so she won't worry that'll actually likely make her do so even more, I suppose I do owe her a return favor. Give me the details."

* * *

A while later, Shane Pawling, casually dressed with a scraggly beard, huddled by an urban street pay phone in a spot several blocks from his apartment wearing a balaclava ski mask pulled down to hide his identity as extra protection as he made the phone call.

Dragenlyte answered the phone. "This is the lady of the house speaking."

"Ma'am I have a message from a person named Toby. Do y'all knows a Toby?"

"What's the message? Are they going to be late returning?"

"Somethin' like that I'm a guessin'. He sayed they wasn't a comin' home 'cause a snowy storm's a comin' and they don' figure to drive in the mess. But he sayed they is safe and has a place to stay fur the night and mebbe tomorry too, basin' it on the weather thay kin keep on a changin' like it do is what he sayed."

"No, this is not acceptable," Dragenlyte shouted. "Tell him he must either drive back here immediately or tell me where they've stopped and I'll have someone drive out and pick them up."

"Can't rightly do that 'cause I don' know where they is. I knowed there was somethin' I shoulda asked him afore I hanged up. Mebbe that was the thing. But they's warm and safe an' figurin' they can make it back in a day or two for sure."

"I won't let them do this to…"

Pawling hung up the phone and hurried away, muttering to himself, "Now I go to my parents empty condo where the Dragon Lady wouldn't know to look for me even if she knew my name."

He passed a woman on the street who shied away from him and looked nervously back over her shoulder when she was beyond him. That reminded him that he was wearing the ski mask so he removed that and walked on with a jaunty air humming "Ding Dong The Witch Is Dead" from *The Wizard of Oz*.

* * *

Later, Marla and Victor came into the living room and found Cindy standing in the empty fireplace looking up the chimney.

"What are you doing, Cindy?" Marla asked.

"I can see the sky up there."

"What did you expect to see?" Victor asked, barely resisting the temptation to add a guffaw.

"The lady said not to make a fire 'cause there's a cover over the chimney, but I don't see one," the littlest Gordon said.

Marla and then Victor stepped into the large space beside Cindy to look up. Toby entered from the dining room.

"See what I mean?" Cindy asked.

"You can feel the cold draft so the top must be open. I wonder if that's a problem?" Marla said.

"If what's a problem?" Toby asked as he bent and stepped in to join them in a tight group in there.

"There doesn't seem to be a cover over the chimney," Victor pointed out to him.

"It must have blown off. It shouldn't be a problem. Maybe it's good luck," Toby suggested.

They all stepped back into the room, checking that they weren't tracking dirt on their shoes.

"Why would it bring good luck?" Victor finally had to ask since that didn't compute for him.

"People often say that about things that happen that they wish didn't but can't change," Toby said with a shrug. "Then other people won't laugh at them because of what happened. Or at least they hope they won't."

"At least Santa can get in when he comes. That's good luck for sure," Cindy said happily.

* * *

It was snowing now in the town of Festivity.

On Tallmann's hill, the highest point in the area, that looked out over the town below, Rudolf Rambler lifted a brightly colored hang glider from the back of his pickup truck.

He made some final adjustments and slipped that onto his back.

He stumbled a bit as he got the feel of the thing and as the wind caught it a bit.

"Congrats, Rudolf. This is surely the best gift I've ever bought for myself. No way I'm waiting until morning to try it out. Besides, if I mess up the first time, nobody'll see me in the dark."

He made a practice run toward the edge of the hill but didn't launch himself. "Gotta get the feel of this first."

* * *

In the Quade House living room, Toby watched as the Gordon kids positioned an inflated air mattress in the fireplace.

Victor said, "I'm telling you, Santa's so experienced at going down chimneys that he never gets hurt except in silly TV commercials."

"But it makes Cindy feel better and it's an extra so nobody has to sleep on it. It doesn't hurt anything so this takes care of the worry," Marla replied.

"Thank you. I do feel better now," Cindy said.

"Then we all do, Cindy," Toby assured her.

* * *

Up on Tallmann's hill, Rambler took a deep breath and then a running start - and launched himself off the edge on the hang glider.

"Oh my gosh, what a sensation! This is wonderful! I'm flying!"

He floated over the town while people went about their business below without noticing him.

He ever so gingerly followed the instructions he had read in the pamphlet and found that indeed he could affect his direction so he made a long curving pass over the terrain.

"I should have done this years ago. Yahoo! Merry Christmas to all!"

Chapter 16

Dragenlyte was alone in the Gordons' condo master bedroom, on the phone, pacing in annoyance with the door closed. The sounds of a sedate party in the living room filtered in.

She said into the phone, "Humbug! If you can't find out for me who can? You're supposed to be able to get me information that's not available to just anyone and all you can tell me is that the call was placed from a pay phone at Fourth and Pistachio streets?"

She disconnected the call with a jab of her finger. She continued to herself, in a mincing tone, "'I narrowed it down quite a lot. I'm a phone company executive, not a private detective'." She switched back to her regular tone. "Why do I bother cultivating these people if they don't come through when I want them to?"

She turned when there is a light knock and Klemper entered in a coat with drops of melted snow on it.

"Oh, it's you. How's the party going? Are the Harbisons happy that they're getting what they want as hosts even if I'm stuck without the brats to show off as my contribution to the spirit of the season?"

"They all are going through the motions so it is a basic success," Klemper reported.

"That's all they should expect - and be glad of that much."

"You vould be glad mit der least part? I think not. I also think they vil not make der mistake of hiring you again."

Dragenlyte picked up a four-inch thick personal address book.

"Who else do I have any influence with that can find out who that dolt was who called so I can find where my nephews and nieces are hiding from me?"

Klemper glanced over a hand-written list on the bed. "If you have called all these, you have asked anyone I know of and some whose names I do not recognize."

"I could forgive the monsters for arriving back late, but I simply know in my bones that this staying away because of a supposed snow storm is a lie, "Dragenlyte grumbled.

"It is for sure snowing outside now."

"A mere coincidence. Mark my word, I'll find them and they'll have dinner with the Charlestons tomorrow and with Austin and my other guests tomorrow evening so help me...whoever."

"You have been big planning this day since der summer. I saw dat when you showed me der first list.."

"Of course. You don't get the best results from almost the last minute plans. You persuade the important people to commit to dates and times well in advance - knowing you'll make sure the others know you had commitments so those who didn't show up to for them to be seen with, caused the problems."

"They are for sure not at your nephew's or at his parents' house. I ruined good shoes confirming that his car is not within three blocks of either residence."

"I need to switch modes. So far I've been using my considerable charm to persuade people to break the silly rules in order to trace that call, now I need to intimidate the ones who can do it."

"Der stick is always stiffer dan der carrot."

Klemper gave her boss a hard look. "I remember how you before tried to trick somebody else to get you vhat you vanted to know from der sources you could not go and check on yourself."

Dragenlyte was startled that Klemper knew about anything like that since she hadn't done that since she hired her.

"I don't know what you can be referring to," Dragenlyte said, hoping to end this topic forever.

"You wanted insider word on some maybe, maybe not coming upper level job changes for to position you mit der likely new vinners but mit no contacts high enough up to know much."

That sounded familiar but had been before she met Klemper, let alone hired her.

Klemper went on, "You offered one executive secretary cash to hear the whispers and rumors but she reported you as maybe doing der insider trading. Der report on dat said you didn't have much money to invest but seemed mostly interested in which coat tails to try to be pulled along by."

"I don't recognize any of that as more than jealous fantasy."

"Twice, maybe more, in a week people higher in the company were seen to chat mit you to be finding out what you know. They say not much. But you are now not safe for dem to be seen mit. You must change companies and social circles. How many think vhat vhen they hear your name no one can even guess. Do you have lists of them?"

"That's silly nonsense. Why would you think you know anything about what I might have done before I became your boss?"

"I checked on you mit many sources before I did more than offer you der canape off a tray at somebody else's party. There vas lots of talk about you. Some seemed like to be accurate. Some vas maybe vhat people misremembered of what you lied or bragged about. Some was for sure put-you-downs by people who don't trust you or like you."

"But you threw all that trash aside and signed on with me."

"For as long as you don't go too far into crazy or cheats. I know I can walk out vhenever I want and be hired elsewhere in an hour but I vould ALWAYS tell officials what I heard and saw as a person if asked."

Dragenlyte debated her response. That was a subtle reminder of their reality, not an open threat. She had used the tactic multiple times herself with others. Be careful and be sure to be generous and it would go no further. But one more factor to consider when she thought about spur of the moment actions or reaction. A nod that she got the message but then move on, Nothing more needed to be said for now.

But yes, she did have to revise some tentative longer term plans to be sure she bought her way out of this relationship without lingering resentment. Which curved back around to today's plans to impress Austin Noble and insert herself into his social set.

"That phone call's the only trail to the children for now. If I knew who made it, I'd get the information I want from him - or his viscera on a platter," Dragenlyte growled.

"Ah, you remind me. Der caterer wants to know what to do mit der leftovers," Klemper said as she headed for the door.

"They go in the fridge in case the children are hungry after I drag them home from the wilderness or wherever they are."

Klemper closed the door behind herself to give the boss privacy to administer a verbal clobbering to whoever could not supply her with the info she wanted when she demanded it.

She punched a number into her phone. There were several tones but they didn't mean anything to her. Then the man she intended to lay into. "Good afternoon, may I ask who is calling please."

"You know what this is and why I'm calling again."

"Is this Ms. Dragenlyte calling?"

"Of course. You don't have caller ID and don't recognize me?"

"Following new directives, I'm requiring you to establish for the official record who you are and what you're calling about. Few people would know how to direct dial this office," he said.

"What's going on?" she asked, angry but now a bit wary.

"Your earlier call from that phone to this number requesting that the company trace a call for you was noted by our monitoring system."

"Too bad..."

"My top superior saw that system alert and called me about it," he went on. "I had to explain to him how our Mr. Andrews called me right before you did and threatened my job. He would get rid of me if I didn't do whatever the woman who called from your number wanted done, all normal rules and regulations ignored. And I'm quoting now - *unless it is so obviously criminal that someone would go to jail over it.* Oh, and there would be a heavy penalty if he wasn't shielded from getting his hands dirty with it."

"That's all your problem, buddy. I couldn't care less about anything except you getting me the traced number I demanded. I'll say the word and you can be sure Jake Andrews will have you out..."

"Not likely," a woman cut in. "I'm Mrs. Zimmer from the phone company security office informing you that we have stepped in and Mr. Andrews is on immediate unpaid leave with the intent to fire him after the holidays. At that time, if we need to, we'll subpoena you to explain yourself to a court. Until then, don't call this employee again. Whether Jake Andrews will have any more to do with you will be up to him."

The call was disconnected.

Ms. Dragenlyte sat down hard on the bed. More mess she couldn't forget about but for now maybe finding and taking control of the Gordon kids was more important than ever.

Chapter 17

Rudolf Rambler smiled ear-to-ear as he trudged himself and the hang glider along a back street in Festivity toward the top Tallmann's hill. He assured himself, "After tonight I'll have a buddy to drive me back up here each time, but I can't stop with just one trip. I'm a bird-man now! I also need to practice the control movements."

At the top, he donned his new toy, adjusted the equipment - and took off over the town again.

* * *

Toby and the three Gordons sat at the dining room table. Toby said, "Okay, we all agree again to stay here for the night. We'll decide about tomorrow tomorrow."

"Assuming that Aunt Sally doesn't swoop in like an eagle and carry us off to dinner with her rich friends," Victor muttered.

"She'd be like a vulture - and she's not friends with them, they only want to use one another when it's convenient," Marla commented.

"Okay, so we agree we need to be cautious then," Toby said. "She'll be looking for us since we're not cooperating with her plans and she has a lot of resources."

"Does that mean guns?" Cindy asked with fear in her voice.

"No, it means people who'll do favors for her like pass along the word if they hear where we are," Toby hurried to reassure the little girl. "No guns or other dangerous weapons are involved in any of this."

"Anybody we meet could be her spy," Victor cautioned.

"Let's not overdo the paranoia, Guys. She's not a mastermind, only a woman who knows how to manipulate people," Toby insisted.

--

"What will she do to us when she catches us? Will it hurt a lot?" Cindy asked with a cringe.

"No, I guarantee she won't hurt you no matter what. She wants to use you in the short-term but she doesn't want to get sued and especially not to get arrested," Toby said.

"Ms. Oily Olive on the other hand might do anything, so don't hesitate to hurt her before she can hurt you," Marla said.

Toby noted, "I needed to be able to rent this house in a hurry without putting up cash I don't have so I used what I knew about her but that means one or two local people know she or people connected with her are here tonight. I hope that won't be a problem but we need to be ready in case people ask about her."

"What should we say if they do?" Cindy asked.

"That she's fine and you have to run along now so you can't talk more," Marla suggested. "The less you say the better."

"But hide if you see somebody dressed like a witch. That might be one of her girlfriends spying for her," Victor said, then giggled.

"We have to consider that she might have friends around here since she knows Mr. Quade enough that he owed her money. So it's best if the local people don't know who we are," Toby said.

"What do you think she'll really do?" Cindy asked.

"She'll try to find out where we are, then drive out here to take you back. That's the bottom line," Toby answered. "No beatings or hard pinches but probably lots of yelling and nasty looks."

"I'll be all right with that. I can pretend not to hear her," Cindy said confidently.

Victor considered saying more but decided not to.

* * *

Rambler was flying over the town again.

This time he was doing more maneuvering and was loving the control even more than the simple soaring.

He made a long sweeping turn - and found himself on a possible collision course with four confused crows as he approached the Quade house. He moved his hands along the control bar to tilt away from the birds as they scattered to avoid him.

But he moved too fast and started to lose his grip. "*Uh oh* to *oh no* in three seconds. I should have read the safety harness instructions before I tried this but I was in a hurry to get airborne. Where's friction when I need some?"

* * *

In the dining room, Toby and the Gordons were getting into it now, all laughing hard.

Victor said, "Maybe she'll send Godzilla to stomp on the town unless we agree to pretend to be her kids for a day."

Cindy giggled, "Or she'll send a space ship to beam us up and take us back home."

"Some of the people I've seen her with might have come off a U.F.O.," Marla said and laughed.

"I can see her trying to sweet talk Santa Claus into taking her along in the sleigh until she finds you," Toby said. "But he won't fall for that."

Victor laughed so hard that he slipped off his chair.

Marla guffawed, "But Victor fell for something."

Above the house, Rambler shouted, "Oh no! Watch out below!"

At the shout that seemed to come from somewhere above them, the four young people looked up startled, unsure what was happening. When there was a noise in the chimney the four of them ran into the living room.

They stared as soot showered down in there.

They heard Rambler say, "Is that it? *Uh oh,* I was afraid not!"

With that the man slid, feet first, down the chimney and landed in a seated position with a thump.

* * *

Rambler hardly has time to exchange startled looks with the others before a spot on the edge of the air mattress blew out and as he sensed a movement and rolled off it, the whole mattress took off and flew around the room with everyone ducking out of the way.

The mattress stopped flying and dropped to the floor rather suddenly - landing on top of Rambler who was still face down on the floor and not sure how much of this he was only imagining.

When something big and with some weight landed on his back he thrashed about and ended up clutching the deflated mattress tightly in his arms. Stunned and confused he asked, "I'm not dead am I?"

"No, but who are you?" Toby asked him.

"I'm Rudolf. Rudolf Rambler."

"You spoiled your surprise," Cindy said with a shake of her head to show she thought that was unfortunate or maybe wrong.

"Honey, I've had enough surprises in the last few minutes to last me a long time."

"Why were you on the roof of the house?" Toby asked.

"I wasn't, I was flying over when I lost my grip." Noting their confusion at that he clarified, "I was using my new Christmas hang glider. Some crows made me slip off it. It's a long story."

"You gave yourself a hang glider as a present? Cool!" Victor said.

"Which you just happened to fall off and came right down this chimney?" Marla asked. Her tone said that she had trouble accepting that, even though she resisted shaking her head that she didn't.

Rambler said, "Correct. When I knew I was losing my grip I tried to land but I couldn't get down fast enough. Thank goodness for that air mattress - and I'll pay for it of course. I could have been hurt bad landing anywhere else. I hoped to at least maybe make a soft landing on somebody's roof. What were the chances I'd go down a chimney?"

"Exactly what we're considering," said Toby, who also found the man's story hard to accept.

"You think I was spying on you? Why would I do that?"

"We're hoping no one knows we're here," Marla said.

"There's a problem about that then. Everybody in town knows you're here," Rambler informed them.

"Oh no," Marla moaned.

"Word spreads fast in a small town," Rambler said with a shrug. "That's right, I'm supposed to tell you about it when I stop in later. I wasn't expecting to be here now. Someone wants to put on a costume and play Santa for you if that's all right."

"Who's planning to do that?" Toby asked.

"It's supposed to be a secret so I promised not to tell. You have to act surprised, but I guess if we asked first there's no real surprise," Rambler said.

"As Mrs. Lapinski says, we can act surprised," Victor suggested.

"But all that would mean a fuss and we're trying pretty hard to keep a low profile," Toby reminded the kids. "Can we discourage any visitors without hurting people's feelings too much?"

"The real Santa will visit of course," Cindy assured them all.

"Of course. I can't promise, but I'll see what I can maybe do about discouraging visitors. They were excited to hear about surprise young visitors at Christmas so it may be too late to cancel them all."

Toby and the kids let it show that they had to accept that.

"We'll appreciate whatever you can do, Mr. Rambler. It's all kind of complicated and we don't want to say too much," Toby said.

"I get that. Right now I'd better go find my present. I hope it didn't break or get stuck in a tall tree," Rambler said.

Rambler left by the front door as Toby and Victor folded up the flattened mattress.

*   *   *

Minutes later Cindy took a test jump on a different rubberized mattress in the fireplace and proclaimed, "This one seems good."

"It's firm but soft since it's filled with plastic foam beads, not air," Toby pointed out.

"Now I won't worry about Santa," Cindy said relaxing.

"Or whoever's the next person to come down the chimney. Mrs. Lapinski was right, strange things do happen in this house," Victor said.

"But we're safe and warm in here and since it's Christmas eve nothing bad is allowed to happen to us," Toby said.

"I hope everybody knows that," Victor whispered.

*   *   *

At that same time, middle-aged Elaine Wurster, dressed warm and to hide her identity, was sneaking around outside the house trying to peek in windows. She talked quietly on a cell phone as she did this.

"If I can stay calm, so can you, Mildred. I won't get reported to the police because nobody inside will know I'm around until I want them to. And then I'll be the one calling in the badges to arrest that woman and finally have my revenge."

She moved in a crouch to the side window of the living room then slowly stood up to peek in that window.

She quickly ducked down again. "Darn it, I can't see through the curtain well enough to tell who might be who in there. No, no, I didn't give myself away."

She went to the back of the house, keenly aware of every crunch noise she made walking on the frozen ground. "Shh! They might hear you, Mildred. I'll tell you when there's something to report."

She crept to the kitchen door where she peeked in its curtained window. The light was on, but she couldn't see anyone in there.

Marla has been looking at the pots and pans in a low cabinet near the door and now she stood up.

The girl's sudden appearance startled Wurster who slipped and almost fell on the frozen surface when she moved too fast.

During that, she dropped the cell phone. She hesitated, in an unsteady condition on the ice, trying to decide whether to stay and find that in the dark or to flee before she was caught.

"Oh saints preserve me!" Wurster stepped over and flattened herself against the wall as Marla cupped her hands around her face to better see out the back door window without opening the door.

When the kitchen light went, Wurster relaxed and took a step forward to search for the phone. She froze when a movement at the window indicated that Marla was looking out the window in the back door again without the glare from the inside light.

Wurster moved slowly as she stepped away to the side to be sure to be out of sight from that window. Then she slowly leaned forward until she could see the window and be fairly certain no one was there any more.

When she was tilted as far forward as she dared to be without falling, she spotted her cell phone on the ground. She bent and grabbed it up and kept right on going, hurrying around the side of the house and out to the street.

On the street, Wurster stopped behind a large evergreen and stared back at the house.

She spoke into the phone. "Are you still there, Mildred? I dropped the phone when I slipped but managed to not fall on an icy spot. No, nobody's chasing me. I can't be sure yet but the word around town is that Sally Dragenlyte is here and once I'm sure she is I'm calling in the police and having her arrested for what she did. She thinks she got away with her cheating but I'll teach her a lesson. This is my chance since she doesn't own the police in this town now. I don't think she does anyway. Dang, that'd be a clinker in my plans. No, I'm sure she has no influence here. Festivity's too Hicksville for her to pay attention to. What do you mean I'm babbling? I'm trying to make it worth your money since you're paying for this call. Mildred? Mildred, are you still there?"

She closed up the phone and put it away, mumbling to herself, "I need an excuse to get inside to be sure it's her before I yell cheater."

Chapter 18

Dennis Handerhan's yard was a neatly cluttered space on the edge of Festivity within sight of the Quade house. A wire mesh goose pen occupied one corner. There was also a chopping area and a stack of firewood, a tool shed, a compost heap, and a waist-high tarp-covered stack of items.

Dennis Handerhan himself was at that moment arranging a short board against a section of tree trunk as a chopping block. A long-handled axe stood nearby. Heathcliff, a mature goose, watched the action from inside the pen.

"I'll make this fast so you won't feel a thing, Heathcliff," Handerhan promised the bird. "They said not to give you a name and treat you like a pet if you were going to be Christmas dinner but it happened and I still need to eat."

He took a dark rag from his pocket and flattened it out. "I'll put this blindfold on you so you won't get scared when you see what's coming. Once it's done we'll both be glad this part's over."

He lifted the axe and took a few practice swings at the board without ever actually striking it. "The chopping block's not wide enough to lay you on it and it's too high to just bend your neck over it so I'll lay you on this board to make it work better. Nobody taught me to do that, I figured that part out on my own. We do-it-ourself-types love the challenge of new things."

He put the axe aside and went to the pen. "It'll be quieter around here once you're...you know. But I bought you for eating and it wouldn't make sense to not follow through."

He walked back to the chopping block and deliberately stood with his back to the bird. "You're just meat, bird. It was your intended fate from the start. I don't even remember how you ended up with a name but the thing I'm remembering is that you're for eating."

The goose honked at him and he put his hands over his ears to block out the sound while he silently tried to resolve to do what he set out to do here.

* * *

The three Gordons stood in the kitchen with Toby as he said, "The refrigerator, oven, and range all work but there's nothing edible in the house so I have to go shopping but I won't leave you here alone."

"Is the big bad wolf gonna get us?" Victor asked in mock fear.

"Are there wolves in this country?" Cindy asked in real fear.

"Toby's worried about Aunt Sally," Marla said.

"Aunt Sally or her lackies," Toby said. "It's because we don't know who might owe her a favor that I don't trust anyone."

"Simple solution is that we'll go shopping with you. You said earlier we'd look for presents for one another anyway," Marla said.

"What's the problem with that?" Victor asked. "Don't you have any money, Toby?"

"Money isn't the problem. Being recognized by someone who might call the Dragon Lady and tell her where we are is my concern," Toby replied. "Mr. Rambler says a lot of folks may have heard we're here, but until they see us many may think it's just a rumor."

"So we'll go in disguise," Marla said.

"We can be Santa's helpers like his elves," Cindy said. "I'd like to play elf."

"But we don't want people to notice us and elves on Christmas Eve might attract attention anywhere except a big city," Toby said.

"I guess that that means dressing like a reindeer's out too, huh?" Victor asked with a laugh.

"I'm tempted to risk that just to see you come up with a reindeer costume," Toby said.

"Let's see what we have in our backpacks that we could use," Marla suggested.

"Mrs. Lapinski said there were clothes in the upstairs closets too," Cindy reminded them.

* * *

Dragenlyte tried to always be prepared when she attended any social event. Doubly so when she was organizing or running things, officially or not. That included an up-to-date potential usefulness rating for each invitee she had been able to hear of and a plan for endearing herself to each.

She had calculated up a storm how to profit the most from the nominal hosts and the guests to this party and those tomorrow and had printed that out on paper for fast reference if she had to decide which of two guests to support in a disagreement. The time to boot up her laptop to check the list could be too long when tempers were flaring.

She didn't risk having that paper on her - and a fancy dress doesn't have pockets for such things. She did though hide it elsewhere in the master bedroom, not with her coat or laptop.

During the party, on one of several trips to be alone for a time to fume and plot revenge because the Gordon children for not being here to play the parts she had intended for them, she found that page partly unfolded in the dresser drawer where she had hidden it, but still folded into quarters.

Had someone read her list? Maybe even recorded it on a phone? Who? A guest? A caterer's worker? The snobbish caterer himself?

At that moment, Klemper came in to give a progresss report on the party. And became the prime suspect, mostly because she was conveniently right there.

"Did you open the dresser drawer?" Dragenlyte asked.

"No."

"I don't like lies."

"Do many you say dat to not laugh right at you as therefore not liking yourself which you do so much? Vhat is der bug in your bonnet dis time?"

"Someone went through things they had no right to touch."

"In a dresser drawer? Und not your dresser drawer."

"I put a sheet of paper folded in quarters in there a while ago. Now I find it partly opened. That must mean somebody took it out, read it, and put it back."

Klemper pulled the not fully closed drawer more fully open. She nodded to herself and barely resisted rolling her eyes. "Clothes packed down tight so hardly room for der paper on top? No. Loose packed so plenty of room for der paper to open part of vay. Case is being closed," she said and slid the drawer closed.

"Maybe. But it could be a snoop and I disapprove of them."

Klemper didn't even resist a mocking laugh as she left.

* * *

Shortly, Toby and the Gordons were dressed in different clothes. Each child wore a scarf that partly covered his or her face and a too large hat that also obscured his or her identity. They were having fun laughing at one another.

Toby looked them over and said, "We'd get failing grades for proper fit but you do look like refugees from a hobo jungle, not those Gordon kids."

"I didn't know hoboes live in the jungle. I might visit them there sometime," Cindy said, always glad to learn new facts.

"But for tonight be content with whatever open stores we can find near here. There may not be many," Marla cautioned.

"Especially ones open on Christmas Eve," Toby added.

"But Mrs. Lapinski said there's at least a supermarket so we can give cans of corn or peas as presents," Victor said.

"Or candy canes and chocolates," Cindy said and smiled.

"I definitely like Cindy's choices better," Toby agreed. "But we have to remember that we're just passing through and don't want to get chatty with anyone. We don't want to lie, but there's no reason we have to give people an opening to ask us personal questions."

"I'll keep an eye on these two," Marla promised.

"And I'll drag her away if there are any dreamy boys in the store," Victor promised in turn.

Marla playfully pulled Victor's hat down to cover his whole head in response. "Wise guy. Wait a few years."

* * *

The Festivity Market was a good-sized standard contemporary full service supermarket. At the door, the foursome stood with a cart as Toby said, "The shelves have been picked over but we should find enough essentials to make dinner and breakfast."

"Plus some candy canes and chocolates," Cindy said.

"I consider those essentials today," Toby agreed. "Look, it'd be faster to split up and each find a few things, but the way so many people are looking at us it's probably best to stay together so we can fend off those with questions."

"You'll be cooking so we need to pick things you know how to make," Marla said to be practical.

"You also have the money so you need to say if we can afford things," Victor added, another practical person.

"Besides, our hats might slip down so we can't see and we might get lost if we're by ourselves," Cindy worried.

Toby nodded. "It's agreed then, we do this together. And we'll keep an eye on you, Cindy. We won't lose you, I promise."

* * *

Thirty minutes later Victor had a reassuring arm around Cindy. Marla and Toby surveyed the bagged items in their cart.

Toby said, "They close at ten tonight and won't restock until day after tomorrow so we had to make do."

"There were still some good choices. We like all of these things," Marla assured her.

"But everybody in the world knew us," Victor whispered.

"They were friendly people though," Cindy noted.

"We need to accept that the word's out that we're related to Aunt Sally but it probably won't make any difference," Toby said.

"We're gonna have a good Christmas, I'm sure of it," Cindy said emphatically because she really was.

"I agree a hundred percent. We mustn't let anything spoil it for us," Toby replied.

"Not even Aunt Sally?" Victor asked.

"Especially not Aunt Sally," Marla said.

"Anyone want to take some money and buy presents? Since we're not hiding, there's no reason you can't. I'll wait with the food."

Toby held out money and each child took some and hurried off into the store.

* * *

Dragenlyte moved through the evening party trying to detect by their smirks and comments to others who might have read her ratings and plans. Her odd behavior amused a few, concerned a few others, and was clearly prompting revisions of her social rating among everyone.

Klemper watched in silence and reconsidered her situation.

* * *

A few minutes later, Toby and the three Gordons walked the cart toward the car.

"Santa will bring more but we have a few things now," Cindy said happily. "Thank you, Toby."

"Yes, thank you, Toby. We'll pay you back when we get home," Marla promised.

"Unless sneaky Olivia stole our money," Victor grumbled. "I just don't trust that woman."

"No problem. It's all part of the special Christmas in Festivity celebration for this year," Toby told them. "Now we're stocked up on food so we can have a late but much appreciated dinner."

"And see if anyone else will drop down the chimney to visit. That includes Santa Claus as a for-sure of course," Victor said.

The others all nodded agreement. The Quade house was one strangely special place.

Chapter 19

Wurster was back outside the Quade house carrying her cat. She said to the animal, "Drat, they were out and now they're back and I didn't get a good look at them to save me this trouble. But at least I know the whole bunch are back inside now so it's snoop time. You've caused me trouble doing this on your own twice, Kitty, so don't you complain about doing it again now."

She moved to look in the side window of the living room but again couldn't see much.

She moved to the arbor and pulled on it to test that it was intact and firmly attached to the side of the house.

She stepped back a bit, stroking the cat, and checked that no one was watching from the street or out the house windows.

"Here goes nothing!" She swung her arms up and sent the poor startled cat flying through the air to land on the roof where it hunched down in terror.

"Now look what you've done, Kitty. Always getting yourself into these problems and I have to rescue you."

With a fair amount of trouble, she climbed up the arbor and prepared herself to go onto the icy roof.

She took an experimental step or two to assure herself that she could navigate up here with caution.

She grabbed up the cat that was too scared to move and carried it to the relative security of the chimney where she could hold on.

She whispered to the animal, "We won't slide around at this spot. Since we're up here I might as well check what can hear what's going on down in the house, right?"

But the chimney was too high for her to look down into easily so she decided to climb up enough to do that.

When it is obvious from some careful testing that she could not climb straight up, she turned her back to it so she could sit up on it, swing one leg up and get up that way.

It was awkward to say the least doing this, especially while she held the appropriately terrified cat by its nape.

"I didn't expect it to be so hard to get up this thing."

The cat wiggled around - and Wurster lost her grip on it.

"Oh no. Kitty!"

The cat fell a short distance down the chimney but was able to grab a ledge in there.

Wurster, hands freed, slid herself sideways onto the top of the chimney.

Seeing the cat not that far below her, she reached for it.

"Hold on, mommy's gonna save you. Oops, no, she's not!"

Wurster slipped into the chimney head first, grabbing the cat as she slid down inside it.

*   *   *

Wurster and the cat landed sprawled on the foam pellet-filled mattress. The living room was empty.

After a long moment, she realized she was shaken and likely in the process of bruising but amazingly was not seriously hurt. She sat, further checked that all her parts seemed to be there and working, then and scrambled out of the fireplace.

Once released, the cat ran out of sight. Its person made a grab for it but it was already out of reach. It would be okay for a while.

Wurster tiptoed to the side of the fireplace and listened. There was a buzz of voices from the kitchen.

She peeked around the fireplace to see that the kitchen door was closed and there was no one in the dining room. That gave her a sense of relief and emboldened her.

The cat mewed from hiding, which reminded her it was here somewhere and needed to be retrieved.

She moved around the room, moving things aside as she searched for and finally was able to grab for the animal that was now actively avoiding her.

Cindy called, "I'll see if I can find it in the living room."

Wurster ducked into the coat closet in the entry.

Cindy entered the living room and stopped when she noticed the furniture that Wurster had moved around. She looked around, more confused than frightened.

Then she noticed spots of water on the floor near the mattress where ice from Wurster's shoes had melted.

She leaned close, picked a small mat of cat hair off the mattress, and held that up to examine it.

Cindy stepped up onto the mattress so she could look up the chimney but saw nothing that told her anything useful.

She walked quietly to look into the entry and was startled when the door to the coat closet moved as it was pulled completely closed. Then the knob slowly turned. The girl silently stepped back out of sight.

After a few seconds the knob turned and Wurster inched the door ajar again to see out. She pushed the door open more and was ready to step out when she heard the voice.

"Who are you?" Cindy asked her.

"Uh, I'm looking for my lost cat. She's not in here so I'll be on my way. Thanks for your help."

Marla called from the kitchen, "Is somebody there, Cindy?"

"A lady who I think came down the chimney with some kind of a furry animal," Cindy called back.

Wurster considered running out the front door, but when Marla came into view still wearing her over-sized hat, Wurster decided she had to check this person out as a top priority.

Marla stopped in the living room and, when she saw Wurster's stare, pulled the hat down farther.

Wurster now moved into the living room to get a better look of this other person.

At a wave from Marla, Cindy ran into the kitchen.

Wurster circled Marla like the girl was a specimen she was trying to authenticate as she said, "It's been a long time hasn't it."

"Who are you and what do you want?" Marla demanded.

"Once a trickster and it stays with you for life it seems."

"Did you really come down the chimney?" Marla asked.

"The years should tell but I have to admit they don't seem to have. But I can't see enough to be sure either."

Toby, Victor, and Cindy hurried in from the kitchen.

Toby said, "Yes, can I help you? I'm in charge here tonight."

Wurster glanced at him but dismissed him with a shrug saying, "Can't be you. Can't be any of you others so it must be her."

As she stepped forward for a closer look at Marla, the girl backed up to prevent that.

"It's time for you to go, whoever you are. This is unacceptable behavior," Toby said loudly.

Wurster tensed and telegraphed her intention to make a grab for Marla's hat, but Victor stepped between her and the girl.

Wurster grabbed the boy and roughly shoved him aside. "Get out of the way and stop protecting that old witch."

Toby now stepped directly in front of Wurster and when she raises her hands to strike out at him he made it clear he would respond in kind. That gave Wurster pause.

Marla pulled off her hat as Cindy ran to and clung to her.

Wurster gasped, "You're not her! Which one of you is she then?"

She looked around convinced one of them must be the person she was looking for but clearly not seeing that person. "I guess you're hiding her then since none of you's the guilty party."

Toby demanded, "Either tell us who you are and what this is about or get out. Victor, the cell phone. Even in a small town I'm sure they'll respond to nine-one-one. We have a home invasion in progress."

Victor ran over and picked up the cell phone on an end table and prepared to punch in numbers.

Wurster telegraphed her move, then made a dash to try to get to Victor but Toby stepped ahead of her and shoved her hard so she fell backwards into a chair.

The startled Wurster said, 'Who do you think you're shoving?"

"A whacko who's babbling and attacking the kids. She has no name but I'll break her bones to stop her," Toby replied.

"This isn't right," Wurster insisted.

Toby replied, "I agree but I'm doing the right thing."

"My name's Elaine Wurster. I'll bet that rings a big old bell to her people."

The others exchanged looks and shrugs. No one knew the name.

"Who's her?" Cindy asked.

"Let's not play games, you know who I mean," Wurster insisted. "Word on the street is that she brought you out here today."

The others frowned as they considered that but it still didn't tell them anything useful.

Then Toby got an idea and asked, "Are you here looking for Sally Dragenlyte?"

"Of course. Not that I really want to talk to her but I'm eager to catch her where she's vulnerable."

"She's not here, we ran away from her," Cindy said.

"Swear on your Christmas candy that none of you is her is some fiendish disguise?" Wurster asked looking from one to the other.

"I don't think any of us as looks fiendish but I admit that if Aunt Sally could make herself look like any of us that would certainly be fiendishly clever," Toby conceded.

"We hope Aunt Sally's back in the city," Marla said. "We came out here to get away from her and her parties."

"Drat. So I went to all that trouble for nothing. Poor kitty, wherever she is."

"Should we know what that means?" Victor asked.

"Years ago and using a fake name, Sally Dragenlyte cheated this town. I caught her in her lies and tried to stop her but when I reported it to the police man on duty he wouldn't do anything about it. She said she was a buddy of the Chief and maybe he believed her. Another of her lies. I swore that when I got my chance I'd get her for that."

"Back then this was a place where she didn't try to buy off the local policeman, just lied to him," Toby said, following that idea.

"What did she cheat you about?" Cindy asked.

"Uh, grown up stuff. The details aren't important now."

"And what does a kitty have to do with any of it?" Victor asked.

Wurster looked around the room. "She's my cat. She's here somewhere. She got spooked falling down the chimney along with me."

"That requires an explanation," Toby insisted.

"She got up on the roof and I climbed up the arbor to get her. Kitty fell in part way when I tried to climb up on the chimney to listen for Sally Dragenlyte's voice. I tried to grab her back out and we both fell down."

"Wow, the mattresses saved two people," Cindy said in awe.

Wurster gave the girl a puzzled look but Toby gestured that they wouldn't bother to explain that.

He said, "We'll keep an eye open for your cat if it's in here. If you leave a number, we'll call if it shows up. But not if Aunt Sally pays an unexpected and unwanted visit, how's that? Or maybe if she does so you can come with the current police."

Wurster wrote a number on a slip of paper and handed it over. "I'd want to know about kitty either way. If the witch shows up I'm even more interested in hearing about it. It'd be great to mess up her book. That'd be the best revenge for what she did to Festivity."

"Again we have no idea what you're talking about," Toby said.

"She had long-term plans for a long time."

Toby shrugged. That didn't tell them anything useful."

"Back then there was a lot of confusion and nobody really in charge with the final word. Ultimately nobody followed through for the town. I learned her identity and started to keep tabs on her. I made it my duty," Wurster said.

"How did you learn who she was if she used an alias when she did whatever she did here?" Toby asked.

"Her license number. She drove her own car here and parked it on the street. When she was gone and the harm was done I found out about that and identified her from State's public records," Wurster said.

"Why did *you* check that, not the police?" Marla asked.

The others nodded that they wondered the same thing.

"They could have. I told them that as soon as I knew there were photos of the car and you could read the license plate. The others chose not to do it. Even after I learned who she was, they didn't want to have a big fuss and they wouldn't put her name in the town's records of the incident,"Wurster said.

"That doesn't make sense," Toby said.

"I agree. But ask anyone who was here eighteen years ago. They won't deny it, they just won't want to talk about it."

"What did you learn that could interfere with a book?" Victor asked.

"She made the mistake several times of bragging to people who wrote about it that for most of her life she's been keeping notes on people and events that she has manipulated and stuff she has gotten away with. She plans in her old age to maybe edit it together and publish it as her tell-all autobiography."

"Does that mean a book about her car?" Cindy asked.

The others all laughed good-naturedly to not embarrass her. She got that but still needed an explanation.

"That's a book about a person's life that they write themselves, rather than one somebody else writes about them," Marla said. "That confused me the first time I heard the word too."

"It can be a way to say the things you wanted to at earlier times but didn't dare. If she ever really stops caring what others say about her, that's a way to have some revenge on those she spent her years flattering and using," Toby said.

"I see lights outside! Is that somebody coming here?" Victor shouted as he ran to the front window.

In a flash his sisters and Mrs. Wurster were beside him, with the curtain lifted for them all to see out.

"Nobody to worry about. That the family that live down the way in their car. Probably were out doing last minute shopping," Wurster said. "I'd better get home and get things unpacked from my own grocery shopping."

"What about your cat?" Cindy asked.

"She won't be a problem when she decides to come out from wherever she's hiding. You have the number to call me."

While the others were thus distracted, Toby lowered his head to look at the floor and said quietly to himself, "My parents and yours have heard those rumors about the Dragon Lady's notes. In recent times they're wondering and worrying that she's picking fights with us to have ammunition in her notes for attacking all the Jansens and the Gordons for not fawning over her enough. They're worried about her trying to use us, especially you kids, to poke around for gossip where she can't be allowed to go."

Chapter 20

As Wurster walked away from the Quade house without her cat, John Febbraro, now tall and imposing if slightly paunchy hunk at forty, emerged from hiding and moved stealthily toward the building.

Looking more scared than scary, he crept onto the porch and peeked in a living room window.

He froze in place as Victor moved the curtain at that window aside to reach through and blindly stick a paper decoration on the glass while looking behind him at something going on in the room.

Febbraro flattened himself against the wall beside the window as Victor turned and inspected his job, the boy's face suddenly on clear view behind the glass.

Febbraro held his breath and stayed still as Victor pressed his face against the window in an attempt to see what might be out there where the man was standing. He called to Cindy, "Is anyone outside on the porch?"

"No, it's cold out there," she answered with a *brrr* for emphasis.

When Victor backed away, letting the curtain fall into place, Febbraro hurried over, climbed over the porch railing and ran to hide in the shrubbery away from the house.

Toby came out the front door and looked along the porch. Then went to the edge to look along the street.

Victor came out behind him and looked along the snow-free porch where a few bits of ice from the grass showed feet had been. He asked nervously, "I can't remember. Was that ice there before?"

"We walked all around and it's so cold so it's probably from our own shoes. No sign of anyone else around," Toby said to reassure him.

"I thought I saw something but now it doesn't seem like there could have been anyone out here," Victor said,

"You did the right thing checking. Keep your eyes open since we all have to look out for one another."

Those two went inside and closed the door behind them.

After a few seconds, Febbraro emerged from hiding, but then he ducked back out of sight as Mrs. Lapinski's car pulled up and stopped by the front walk.

* * *

Mrs. Lapinski stood in the living room in her coat and hat with the four overnight tenants.

Toby assured her, "We're stocked with food now, thanks."

"We were surprised that everybody seemed to know who we are," Marla admitted.

Mrs. Lapinski laughed. "There are no others as young as you left in the town right now so you're celebrities. The grandchildren come to visit but that will be tomorrow afternoon. Many of us older folks want so much to have one of the parties again. Without youngsters laughing and happy they don't feel the same. We could put something together although it wouldn't be fancy with no planning ahead."

Toby hadn't wanted to ask this but knew he must. "Did you stop by to invite us to a town party of some sort."

"Goodness, didn't I say that first? Yes, a group of the town folks want to throw a Christmas eve party for you. The phones have been ringing off the hooks since you were seen at the supermarket," she said.

Cindy sadly shook her head - cuing her siblings to do the same.

"That's very nice of you all but we plan to try out a new holiday traditions with just a small group celebration tonight. And we're a bit concerned about unexpected visitors or surprises,"Toby said.

This time Marla was the cuer and the three Gordans nodded agreement with Toby - and smiled in anticipation.

"That's fine. We knew you might have plans. That's why I came to check before people did much about this." She glanced around as if checking for eavesdroppers, then said quietly, "Many of us wonder if one town lady might keep a certain woman with an unpleasant history with the town in the past aware of everything that happens here. The local woman, known to all as a snoop and snitch, talks about the other woman so often that we wonder if that's to cover that she's her spy."

"That's the kind of person we're concerned about," Toby said. "I hope you'll all understand that we made plans before we got here."

"Oh, how about this? Would it be okay if just one man, one with a white beard and bag of presents, stops by in a little bit?" Mrs. Lipinski asked, excited by this alternative.

Toby looked at the Gordons, not sure what to say.

"You'll know it's only Bobby so he won't be unexpected. This is exactly the right night of the year for this," Mrs. Lapinski said with a hint of a pleading tone.

"We're waiting for Santa Claus," Cindy told her.

"Exactly. He'd like so much to do it. He's never had his turn. It was always his father's job and then things changed and there were no children around," the woman said.

"Who's Bobby?" Victor asked.

Mrs. Lapinski said, "My son. Bob Lapinski. He has the old Santa suit and wants so much to bring some joy with it."

"Oh, if it's your son we'll know who it is even though we'll also recognize him as St. Nick. That'll be okay won't it, Kids?" Toby asked.

"Sure. We'll make it a new Christmas tradition to be visited by as many Santas as are around," Victor said happily.

As they stood in the doorway and waved as Mrs. Lipinski got in her car, Toby said, "I can't be sure but I'm comfortable thinking that at this moment Aunt Sally doesn't know where we are. I'd be happier and feel safer is I thought she doesn't care, but from all I know about her I can't go that far."

* * *

As Mrs. Lapinski's car disappeared in the distance, Febbraro emerged from hiding and hurried across to the trellis. He now fairly obviously carried something large under his coat.

He checked the soundness of the trellis, then climbed it to the top, hesitating before he pulled himself up onto the roof itself. The objects under his coat were a hindrance.

Moving carefully, wary of icy spots, he climbed onto the roof and across it to the chimney.

He held onto the chimney for support while he waited for his heart to stop pounding so fast.

He whispered to himself, "This could easily be misunderstood and ruin my holidays but if I'm careful nobody should ever know what I did. I'm glad to find the cover gone so I don't have to debate whether to remove it or scrap my plan. I'll be sure to find it and put it back on after the holidays. Here goes nothing."

Keeping a hold on the chimney, he assessed the best spot and the best way for him to climb up on it.

He placed the objects - an eighteen-inch long by eight-inch wide flat board, several lengths of rope, and two large distorted-S shaped metal rods, each with a wide U-shaped side that would fit over the top of the chimney wall, the other a narrow one - on its flat top edge.

He stood for moment silently rethinking whether to do this, then shrugged and decided it was a go.

He moved around the chimney a bit to get away from where the equipment sat, then turned his back and hoisted himself up to sit on its top edge. Moving slowly and cautiously so he wouldn't slip, he swung his legs over and let them hang down inside the chimney flue opening.

Only now did he look down inside. He took a small flashlight from a pocket and shined its bright beam down the flue, examining the walls from top to bottom as much as he could see.

Good, no signs that they intended to build a fire. That would certainly be a problem.

He focused on a narrow ledge about five feet down from the top and shined his light beam all around that. He slipped the wide-U arm of each distorted metal rod over opposite narrow sides of the rectangular chimney wall, looped a tied rope over the narrow U-arm of each, and fitted the other ends of the ropes into notches on the flat board.

Satisfied that the pieces were securely together, he lowered the board down the length of the ropes.

Finally he lowered himself out of sight down into the chimney, holding tight so he wouldn't slip.

After a bit of adjusting in there, he was sitting securely if maybe not especially comfortably on the board, suspended several feet down in the chimney where he could prop himself up a bit by putting his feet on the ledge.

He checked his watch and sat back. What he expected to be the hard part was over and it had gone pretty much as he had hoped and expected. He wouldn't argue if people wanted to say his plan was crazy, but he was doing it.

Chapter 21

Cindy silently led Victor by the arm across the living room to the fireplace and pointed to the new bits of soot scattered across the foam-filled mattress they had placed back in there after checking it for damage.

She whispered, "I heard a noise up in there but I'm afraid to see what it might be."

"Probably just the wind. Let me show you what to do." He called, "Is there anybody up there in the chimney? Identify yourself."

He was more startled than Cindy when there was a response.

"Uh hello. Yeah, I'm up here. Don't mean you no harm. Guess I should come down there and explain. Strange story I realize."

Cindy ran and got Toby and Marla while Victor waited for the stranger in the chimney to descend.

* * *

Shortly, Toby and the three Gordons watched as Febbraro stepped across the mattress into the room, most parts of his chimney seat in hand. "Uh, hi. I'm John Febbraro. I live not far from here. Uh this thing is the seat I made so I could hide in this chimney."

"Why?" Victor beat the others in asking.

"See it's Christmas eve so I didn't want to be at home when my relatives arrive."

Toby was having trouble accepting this. "You planned to hide in somebody else's chimney on a makeshift seat?"

"That was my idea. I didn't expect there to be anybody here."

"Won't your family miss you?" Cindy asked.

The man gestured that this was the long story part of this.

"Sure will. Every year these cousins show up without ever being invited, eat everything in the place, then move on without even a thank you. I've gotten pretty annoyed about it."

"Can't you just tell them not to come?" Victor asked.

"I tried but they came anyway. They don't pay much attention to me," Febbraro admitted.

"That explains why you'd try to fake them out by not being home when they show up anyway," Toby conceded.

"I always loved celebrating Christmas until five years ago when they started dropping in for that one day each year and making it a disaster for me."

"You look cold," Marla said to him.

"We made cocoa. Would you like some?" Cindy asked.

"That'd be nice if you're sure you have enough for everybody. I'm not trying to be a nuisance like them myself on anybody," Febbraro said shyly.

"You guys take our visitor in the kitchen and warm him up while I take care of some details," Toby suggested.

* * *

Sally Dragenlyte moved through the party watching for smirks or those who looked away and wouldn't meet her glare-tinged stare. Who knew more than she wanted them to - that she could use this occasion to punish? She didn't identify anyone.

But as Klemper noted and warned, her employer was rerated downward by a significant number of the guests for her seemingly baseless aggressive attitude.

* * *

Toby, coat on, stood alone on the porch making a cell phone call. "Shane, good friend, how's it going? Any special problems?"

"I'm in my parents condo across the street from where you-know-who is throwing a party. I can see the guests from this window. Can't stretch things to call them revelers. All very proper and sedate. I'm also stretching things to describe it as a party. Maybe when I'm old and mature it'll seem like more," Pawling replied.

"So you got the message to her okay?"

"She wasn't happy but I made the call from a street pay phone, then ran like the devil was after me – which I'm not a hundred percent sure isn't the fact."

"Can you see if she's there? Relax, relax. I don't want you to do anything except see if you can spot her from where you are so I know her location."

"It's good that you explained yourself fast, Toby, my friend. I was halfway to the door heading for Mexico at the thought of being asked to go near her. No, I can't see anybody I recognize as her and I have good binoculars focused on the living room. That high up they don't bother with curtains."

"That's worrisome," Toby muttered.

"Before you ask, no I won't stay here and watch for her. I'm spooked. I'm spending the night with people you don't know where no Dragon Lady would look for me even if she tortured you for hints."

"Would you please, please, please take your cell phone in case I need to reach you? Triple please means it's really, really important or I wouldn't ask," Toby said. "Wow, a double really situation."

"I won't make any promises about that. If I thought she could read my mind through that device I'd pitch it in a minute."

"Okay. I understand. She spooks most of us most of the time. I won't put you on the spot but if I need to, I'll try your numbers to see how safe you're feeling. I promise I'll make this up to you, Shane."

"I have it written in big letters in my little who owes me payback notebook, so I won't forget."

* * *

Ms. Dragenlyte was distracted and that angered her. She had planned this Christmas eve afternoon party weeks ago to be a major event for her to make contacts and impress important people with connections. She wasn't doing any of that.

Worse still, she knew - even as she tried to deny it to herself - that she was making many bad impressions, not simply not making good ones, as she fumed about not being able to salvage the evening with the happy pretend grandchildren children she had promised. She should have hired that troupe of young actors and risked having one or all of them upstage her.

She was supposed to smile but Kempler had twice in the last ten minutes passed by with a tray of canapés as an excuse to warn her she was scaring the guests and those paying to be the designated hosts. Klemper suggested that it would do the least damage for her boss to get out of sight since she wasn't actress enough for this situation. And no, she was often not a good judge of that and certainly not right now.

* * *

The three Gordons and Febbraro got up from the dining room table, leaving the cocoa cups, and began to carefully search the room.

Marla said, "Remember that it's scared so don't try to grab it right away. We only want to find where it is."

"It'd help to know what it looks like," Victor said.

"It's fluffy and brown with some stripes. Medium sized, I guess. I'm not an expert on house cats," Febbraro admitted.

Cindy got down on the floor to look under furniture. "I don't see it anywhere."

"Next we'll look in the living room," Marla directed.

As the four people went into the living room by one door, the cat went into the dining room by the other to hide from them.

* * *

The four repeated the search in the living room.

Victor ran to look behind one piece of furniture after another.

"You're gonna keep it too scared to ever let us find it by running around like that. Slow down," Marla said.

Cindy got on the floor to look under things in here too. Marla stood by her waiting for her report.

"I see some dust bunnies but no fluffy brown cat," Cindy said.

"How many mice do you see under there?" Victor asked.

Cindy sat up in a hurry. "What mice?"

"There are bound to be some in a house in the country like this. They're common aren't they, John?" the boy asked.

"Common and quite harmless. But with no food stored here and the heat at a minimum most of the time they're not likely."

Then to reassure Cindy, he said, "Did I emphasize that they're harmless? There are only nasty ones in cartoon movies."

"Darn, I wanted to see one," Cindy said.

That evoked a big laugh from Febbraro. He had misread the girl and was delighted by her sense of adventure.

Marla commented, "The cat doesn't seem to be anywhere here. Maybe it went upstairs."

"More likely it ducked out the door when Toby went out. This isn't it's home so it'd want to escape," Febbraro noted.

Toby entered by way of the front door, taking off his coat. "Did I hear my name mentioned? What did I do this time?"

"We just wondered if the cat slipped out with you when you went outside. We can't find it in here," Marla explained.

"I didn't see any sign of it but I can't say for certain it didn't," Toby conceded.

"Did you find out for sure where Aunt Sally is?" Victor asked.

"Sort of. I know the party's going on in your condo so I assume she's there racking up social points. That means we can relax and get into the spirit. We need to put up the decorations we bought. They're not a lot but they'll make it more festive."

"Uh, can I make a suggestion?" Mr. Febbraro said.

"Sure, what is it, John?" Toby asked.

"I have a big tree and boxes of decorations for it that I planned to put up day after tomorrow when I was sure my cousins were gone. Why don't we bring those over here and set up that tree in this room?"

"Suppose your cousins show up while we're there?" Marla said.

The man laughed and said, "I guess I'll have to tell them to go fly a sleigh. And I'll actually tell them to do it this year."

They all laughed now.

* * *

Ms. Dragenlyte sort of cut her losses but staying at the side of the room glaring around. Guests now only had to not go near her, they didn't have to move away to avoid her. Had she been able to listen in, she might have been surprised, although not thrilled, at the range of reasons to which people were attributing her current behavior. A whole catalog of snicker-inducing rumors. And the range of assessments about how safe she could be from nasty consequences of what she could deny but not erase from the reality of her past.

* * *

John Febbraro's house was similar to the Quade House but with lots of outdoor light decorations. A large cut fir tree stuck out the back of Febbraro's van. Toby's car was parked nearby. Toby, Febbraro and the three Gordons were busy packing cartons of decorations in the van.

"I enjoy the lights but for tonight I didn't expect to turn them on at all," Febbraro said. "It's a shame to do it but I'll turn them off when we leave."

"That's a really nice tree, Mr. John," Cindy told him.

"It'll look especially nice when you've all helped decorate it," he agreed.

"We put lights in our windows but we don't have any on the outside since we live on the fifteenth floor," Cindy said.

"There are lots of lights on the stores and the street lamps and all though," Victor explained.

An old car pulled up and Febbraro's cousin Dwayne, his wife Mindy, and their three children (who looked less than delighted to be here) piled out. Febbraro went over to them.

Dwayne said, "How's that for good timing? Looks like we arrived just in time to watch you carry the tree inside, Cousin."

"Uh no, the tree's on its way elsewhere, Dwayne," Febbraro said.

"Well me and the family can tag along and be part of the party wherever," Dwayne said, not the least put out.

"No, I'm not in the entertaining business any more. You and the family'll have to go find yourselves a motel for the night and some restaurant for your meals. Or maybe give her a call and arrive earlier than usual at your mother's. Also, in the future, you need to always call and get an invitation before you make the trip this way. Oh, and have a nice Christmas."

Febbraro walked to Toby and the Gordons by his van without giving the relatives a chance to argue.

Dwayne and Mindy had words by their car while their children watched with concern, then gradually with bigger and bigger smiles of delight.

"Will this ruin Christmas for those kids?" Cindy whispered.

"It shouldn't," Febbraro responded at the same volume. "They don't want to be here but they have no say in it. They want to get on to their grandma's which is still a two hour drive from here."

"Why don't they go there without bothering to stop here first then?" Victor asked quietly.

"Because Grandma won't let Dwayne drink his eggnog with rum in it and get half-plastered but I would," Febbraro admitted.

"You wanted him to get drunk?" Marla asked.

"No, but I didn't think it was my business to tell him what not to do when I knew he'd do it anyway. I was afraid to make it even less pleasant for the kids by fighting with their dad on Christmas Eve."

"What changed things this year?" Toby asked.

"You folks. This year I have something else to do and somewhere else to be so I can say no without guilt. Don't be fooled though, they won't stay in a dirty cheap motel and eat Christmas dinner at a fast-food place. They have plenty of money but Dwayne seems to get satisfaction out of free-loading even though it embarrasses the rest of the family."

"They're getting in their car," Victor reported.

"The kids are smiling," Cindy added.

"Smiling big smiles too, not just okay ones," Vince said.

"That means Mindy said she'd driving on to Grandma's right now whether he goes along or not," Febbraro explained.

As the relatives drove away, everyone waved to the people by the van - except Dwayne who was a sour-puss.

Febbraro said with a sigh of satisfaction, "Since that problem's resolved I'll leave the lights on all night. I really like to see them."

"John, your relatives stopped two blocks up," Victor reported. "What does that mean?"

"That's Mindy doing the right thing and calling ahead to warn Granny they'll arrive a day early. She wouldn't drive and call at the same time and Dwayne would refuse to make the call," Febbraro said.

Chapter 22

The three Gordons and Febbraro admired the tree now set up in one corner of the Quade house living room with boxes of ornaments stacked by it.

"Yes indeed, it looks fine there," Febbraro said happily.

"You picked a nice one, John," Toby congratulated him.

"You must be a Santa's helper from way back," Cindy said.

"I won't tell you the number but I've selected trees for quite a few years. Decorated each one of them too," the man said proudly.

"With all these ornaments it's gonna be one great looking tree," Victor said as he looked over the boxes.

"With these other decorations too the whole house will be extra special," Marla agreed.

Toby came in from the dining room and said, "Does anybody want any popcorn after we went to the bother of buying it?"

Marla, Victor, and Cindy shouted in unison, "I do."

Then Cindy looked concerned. "But we don't have a microwave here. Was there one in the kitchen?"

"Popping corn's easy on the stove as long as you keep it moving so it doesn't burn. I'm an expert," Febbraro assured them. "Come on, I'll show you how it's done."

Febbraro and the kids headed for the kitchen. Toby put on his coat, took his cell phone, and went out onto the porch.

On the porch as he punched a number into the phone, then as he waited he whispered to himself, "Here goes nothing. I hope this won't be my biggest mistake of the day."

"Hello, this is Austin Noble speaking."

"Merry Christmas, Mr. Noble. How are you this fine night?"

"Mildly curious but not intrigued by this game for long. Who is this?"

"My name's Toby Jansen. I work at Marston and Willow. We've spoken in the office more than once."

"Ah yes, Toby Jansen. Oh, that makes you a relative of Sally's doesn't it? Does she have you checking up on me?"

"Actually it's the other way around. I'm trying to find out where she is."

"Is there an emergency? I'm sure she has a cell phone although like all of us she turns it off sometimes."

"No, no emergency. This is a surprise kind of thing so I can't contact her but I'd be better able to pull this off if I knew exactly where she is so she doesn't walk in unexpectedly and spoil the fun."

"Last I heard from her, she was playing hostess at a party in the city. That wasn't too long ago. She said it was all going well but I could hear in her voice that something she didn't want to tell me about isn't."

"She didn't mention any change of her plans or things not going as intended?"

"Toby, are you in some sort of trouble with your aunt? I won't rat you out."

"I think it's safe to say I'm not her favorite relative. Especially not right now."

"Has this something to do with the Gordon children?"

"What have you heard?"

"Instant concern. Interesting. I suppose I'd better not ask how you've changed her plan to show me how well she interacts with young children at dinner tomorrow."

"You know about that? She told you her game plan?"

"She didn't tell me and would deny it if I mentioned it but I can read between the lines."

"So you're okay with it?"

"I'm flattered that she's willing to go to such lengths to impress me even if she's a bit devious about it. Heck, I know she's not exactly a straightforward lady but I'm not Joe Simplicity myself. What can you tell me about the situation?"

"The kids are with me and she doesn't know where we are."

"Wow, you are an operator! You literally stole them away from right under her nose?"

"With her consent - after a fashion. She told us to get lost for a while so she could set up the party in the Gordon's condo and we did."

"Have you considered how frantic she must be?"

"She might be furious, but not frantic. I got a message to her that we're safe but reluctant to travel in the snowstorm moving into the area."

"Is she such of an ogre that the kids needed to escape her?"

"I'll just say that she's a user and the kids resented being pawns in her plans on Christmas."

"I'd like to meet these kids."

"I'm sure you will but if I can keep a step ahead of Aunt Sally it won't be until at least December twenty-sixth."

"But if I met them first, I could better judge her performance when she introduces me to them. Why don't you invite me to meet them tonight? I give my word of honor that I won't let her know where I'm going or why."

"I don't know. It's super important to our plan that she can't find us until Christmas is over."

"Why?"

"It's not part of the plan to ruin her dinner tomorrow, only to keep the kids from being used as pawns at it."

"Okay, I understand your reluctance to trust me. Do you by chance know how far Crafter is from the city? I'm on the road and I forgot my map and I'm sort of lost and hungry."

"You're in Crafter?"

"Coming up to it. Oh my, is that a problem? Will I possibly be lost forever in the hills?"

"Actually we're not far from there."

"Oh, then I should keep going full speed and not even look around."

"Let's think about this for a minute," Toby said.

* * *

Minutes later Toby went inside and closed the door behind him.

Fred Quade then came out of the shadows and walked by the house with his collar turned up, his hat pulled down, and his head low.

At the edge of the property he ducked into the yard and hurried to the shadows by the side wall of the house.

Cindy called to Toby, "We made enough popcorn to put some on strings to decorate the tree like in the olden times."

Toby replied, "I wondered if we'd have enough to do that. I was afraid you'd eat it all."

"The others are popping some more. There's plenty to eat and use to decorate," Cindy assured her.

Quade checked the strength of the trellis. He and ducked when Cindy moved the curtain at the nearby side window to look out.

He peeked, and seeing that she was still there, edged toward the back of the house to be out of sight. He stayed bent over to be as inconspicuous as possible.

Cindy called, "There's somebody outside, Toby."

"Again? Let me check." Toby went outside and to the end of the porch to look along the side of the house but Quade was out of sight around the back by then.

Toby shrugged and went back inside. "I think maybe it was a dog going through the yard. There's nothing out there now anyway."

"Oh. I couldn't tell what it was," Cindy said, sounding reassured.

Quade tiptoed back to the trellis, checked that it was safe, and carefully climbed to the roof.

Suddenly Toby hurried back out the door and down the porch as if expecting to catch someone snooping there this time. Quade was lying prone on the roof not moving.

Toby went back inside saying, "It probably *was* only a dog."

* * *

As Quade climbed to the top of the roof and proceeded to the chimney, he slipped on an icy spot and frantically threw himself spread-eagled on his belly to clutch the roof.

Slowly he made the rest of the trip to the chimney on hands and knees, happily clutching the bricks when he got there.

* * *

Dennis Handerman had a cup of steaming coffee in hand as he surveyed the way he has rearranged things in his yard. He had laid a six-foot long board over two makeshift saw horses.

"That should do it better. Sometimes taking the time for a cup of coffee pays off."

Determined to get this done without thinking about it too much, he grabbed the goose from its pen, carried it to the board and awkwardly tied its wings to its body with a wide rag strip.

Then he tied its feet together with another strip.

Finally he blindfolded the protesting bird with a cloth strip.

He laid the big bird's whole body on the board with its neck stretched out toward the end and loosely tied the ends of the blindfold strip around the board to keep its head down.

"I'm not enjoying this either. Maybe I should have had the butcher do this part but it's too late for that now. It's now or never, Heathcliff."

* * *

Quade tilted his head over the chimney trying to hear sounds from below but found he couldn't do so while standing on the roof.

After a moment of hesitancy, he climbed up onto the chimney so he was kneeling on the edge, leaning across and looking down the opening - and holding on as well as he could.

He tilted his head and closed his eyes to concentrate on the sounds from below.

* * *

On top of Tallmann's hill Rudolf Rambler launched himself out over the Town of Festivity again in his hang glider.

He sailed out over the town with a little whoop, showing better form and control this time.

"Each trip is a new adventure!"

* * *

In his yard, Handerman hefted the long-handled axe as he took a final look at the bird trussed on the board.

He was pulled up short because the axe had caught in a loop of thin rope running along the ground and between the legs of the saw-horse near the goose's head.

He shook the axe handle to rid it of the rope and in one quick, determined motion closed his eyes and raised the axe overhead.

The rope, still looped around the axe despite his shake to free it, was pulled taut by this action. Then the far sawhorse fell over.

This dropped the end of the board with the goose tied to it to the ground, leaving the other end raised on the other sawhorse with more than a foot protruding beyond the support.

Eyes still tightly clenched closed, Handerman brought the axe down - inadvertently turning it so the side of the blade, not the edge, hit the end of the board a solid whack and he followed through all the way to ground level.

This snapped up the other end of the board, the poorly tied rag strips came loose - and the still blindfolded goose went flying high through the air in a long arc.

Handerman opened his eyes and looked around in confusion. What happened? Where did the bird go and how did things get on the ground like this?

* * *

The goose, now able to use its wings but unable to see, was propelled over housetops in confusion.

Rambler was all smiles as he executed a smooth sweeping turn. Then he saw a blindfolded goose coming right at him.

He slid to one end of the control bar and narrowly missed the goose - but fell off into the top of a tall evergreen tree.

* * *

Up on the roof of his house, Quade was leaning forward, butt in the air, trying to hear.

A noise made him look up - just as the goose banged into him and the two of them tumbled down the chimney together.

He only had time to exclaim, "What? This isn't possible! Whoa!"

Chapter 23

Cindy was the only one in the living room when Quade and the goose hit the mattress in the fireplace hard.

The mattress exploded from the impact and sent small plastic foam pellets over everything on one side of the room, flocking the tree, a chair, the drapes, and some boxes the decorations had been in. Cindy was on the other side of the room and didn't get any on her.

She stared in wonder as the goose, now freed of blindfold and all restraints, recovered from its shock and started to run around the room honking in distress. Quade wasn't hurt but was too shocked to move more than to test that nothing was broken.

Cindy whispered to herself, "The others may not believe this."

The goose stopped and stared for a long moment, then with loud indignant protests, it hurried into the dining room by one door - with Mrs. Wurster's cat chasing after it.

The noise brought Febbraro, Toby, Marla, and Victor on the run. They entered by way of the door the animals had just exited - after a hesitation to see what that movement of smaller bodies was about.

They stared at the flocked tree and furniture - and especially at the man sitting in the fireplace.

They stared, then laughed as the cat came racing in from the dining room through the other door with the angry goose now in hot pursuit of it.

When the cat hid out of reach behind the sofa, the goose flapped its wings to let it be known it was satisfied it had set things right.

"Fred? What happened here?" Febbraro asked.

Cindy said, "I saw it. That man got goosed."

That got startled reactions from the others.

"He what?" Marla asked.

"I got knocked down the chimney when that goose flew into me," Quade explained.

"Are you all right? Is anything broken?" Toby asked.

"My pride's bruised but there doesn't seem to be any physical damage," Quade said as he struggled to his feet. "Thank goodness that I bought that mattress and kept it around."

"It was to protect Santa Claus," Cindy said.

"I don't think he comes down headfirst so he should be all right even without a landing pad. We'll just toss that," Quade said. Then suddenly cautious he whispered, "Where is she?"

"The goose?" Cindy asked.

"The cat?" Marla asked.

"The girls are both here," Toby pointed out.

Febbraro asked, "What were you doing on your own roof where you could fall down the chimney, Fred?"

"I... I was checking for something," Quade answered.

"Maybe listening to find out if a particular lady was in the house?" Toby suggested.

"Yes, I admit it," Quade said.

"This gives a literal new meaning to eaves-dropping. Aunt Sally should be proud to be so much on people's minds," Toby said.

"Aunt Sally sent him?" Victor wasn't following this.

"No, but I'm betting that like Mrs. Wurster she's the one he was trying to find out about" Toby ventured.

"Elaine Wurster's here?" Quade asked looking around.

"She dropped in, lost her cat, and left again," Marla said.

Quade looked from one to the other in confusion.

Toby explained, "She was here looking for Sally Dragenlyte. You are too aren't you?"

Quade was instantly interested. "What's she doing here? Anything illegal we can catch her at? Anything I can use against her?"

He realized he should be careful what he said in front of the kids. "Uh, that is… Uh."

"I've heard from my family that you've had dealings with her in the past which is why you feel you owe her money. I have an idea for finally settling that sneaky debt," Toby said.

Quade nodded in agreement, "She tricked me and I resented it but it was a legal debt so I was stuck. She didn't want the money right then, she wanted to keep me on a string so she could use me when it would be more convenient for her."

"You can relax, she's not here and we don't expect her," Toby said. "In fact we hope she doesn't know we're here and we want to keep it that way. I'll explain my idea in private as soon as we have a minute."

"I'm relieved to know she's not here since I wanted to know if she was but not to deal with her. Where is she?" Quade asked.

"That's a good question. I assume she's in the city at my young cousins' apartment but to find out for sure I'd have to contact her and I'm trying to avoid doing that," Toby replied.

"Wherever she is, she's probably plotting something. That's her way," Quade muttered.

"That's a common thought," Febbraro said.

"Do the bricks in the fireplace with dates carved in them mean something special?" Marla asked, prodded by Cindy.

They all looked at the fireplace.

"I carved those to remember dates when unusual things I couldn't understand at the time happened," Quade said.

He stopped, looked at the floor, and seemed to become sad.

The others looked from one to another, fearing this was a topic best left alone. They all stayed that way for a long moment.

Quade shook himself out of his reverie and was embarrassed when he saw the expressions of concern on the others.

"Whoops, sorry, those things happened back when my wife was still with me and I miss her a lot. But what happened here didn't hurt her or anybody. Didn't even break anything into pieces except my silly pride because I couldn't explain things."

"The kids just saw the carved bricks and pointed them out. You don't owe us any explaination," Toby said.

"They're reminders of interesting events that happened here that I can't understand but the more people I tell about them, the more chance that somebody'll be able to explain them to me."

The Gordons silently gesture-cued Toby to say more.

"Of course we'd like to hear about the mysterious events as long as they're not murder mystery kinds," Toby said.

The Gordons and Febbraro gave him thumbs-up for that.

"The first time it was three pigeons," Quade said.

"Here inside your house?" Cindy asked in surprise, then glanced around worried she should have stayed quiet.

Quade gave her a reassuring wave as he said, "Right here in this room. But they weren't the only unusual living things here that day. My wife's cousin had been brought for a visit. She was in a sad condition after having a stroke. She was in a wheelchair and most of the time didn't seem to notice anything around her."

"We're sorry to hear that," Marla felt she should say for all.

"But it turned into a good day for her when three pigeons came fluttering around the room as she turned to see them and laughed."

"They came down the chimney?" Toby asked.

"That's the mystery. Definitely the cap was off so we could light a fire if we wanted. But also the windows in here were open since we were cleaning them before she arrived. There was soot inside the fireplace as if something brought it down with it or them."

"Several ways for small birds to get in," Victor noted.

"Then what I can't explain. The birds and soot disappeared up the chimney as if being sucked by a strong force. I saw it happen. Or think I did. The invalid cousin and I were the only ones in the room so the only ones who saw any pigeons come or go. I was the only one who could describe what I still am convinced happened," Quade said.

Toby started to ask something, hesitated, then asked quietly, "Did you look for evidence of damaged birds outside?"

"First thing I did," Quade said. "Not even a loose feather."

Febbraro nodded and said, "I have no answer for it but I've heard him tell about it twice before in exactly that way. At the least he has his story settled.

"What about the second brick," Marla asked to move it along.

"The dirty drone lady," Quade said.

"This house has attracted more than its fair share of nasty women for short visits over the years. Ramona had to compensate for a lot - and did it so nicely," Febbraro said.

"Ramona is my wife forever. And she deserves every accolade those lucky enough to meet her want to share."

"The dirty drone woman Helga Harpy was no lady. One who liked to cause messes just for the fun of irritating everyone else. May she rotate in her grave for centuries," Febbraro grumbled.

"In this instance she came to town with an expensive drone back when few knew what they were and dumped loads of ashes down people's chimneys to confuse the home owners who at first didn't know how that happened and who did it," Quade said.

"Then she came to do that here," Febbraro said. "I saw the last stage of it for myself."

"But understand, I didn't know what she was doing and didn't do anything to cause what happened her," Quade said. "It was like my house was protecting itself."

"Tell us what happened!" Marla shouted, then quickly gestured an apology that that came out louder than it should have.

Febrraro gestured that Quake should tell it. "She flew the drone over this house but as it got above the chimney I'm told the flying mini-dumptruck was shoved aside by an air blast or something invisible. It was shoved hard or long enough that it smashed and broke on a branch high in a tree down the street."

"Then the part I witnessed," Febbraro said with a chuckle. At a wave from Quade he finished the story. "She climbed up there to retrieved her expensive harassment tool. Pulling on it from below she caused it to release the ashes, which fell down over her - causing her to try to wave them off so she fell, and broke both her arms when she hit the ground."

"Then the pulled-loose drone hit her on the head," Quade said. He was trying not to let too much glee show. Yes, it's true that she could have been killed, but she was the only one involved."

"I get why you'd make a monument about that," Toby said.

"Was there a third brick story?" Cindy asked.

"There is. That one is the strangest in some ways since I can't figure who, if anyone, did anything to bring it on or got satisfaction from it. I think of it as the big wind blessing," Quade said.

"You're a good storyteller, Mr. Quade. Nifty titles," Toby said.

The Gordons and Febbraro all nodded and applauded.

"My Ramona liked me to make up stories to amuse her. Anyway, in this case that really happened, things start in a neighboring town where some local people made a whole new homemade steeple for their church with a historic early colonial cross on top as a special feature.

"They made that inside a barn and only moved it outside the night before the dedication ceremeny when a crane would lift it into place and the workers would nail it down.

"In the morning when they all gathered for the ceremony a strong wind gust lifted it up and blew it all the way here and sat it down on top of my chimney, the old cross standing over everything. Luckily it was warm weather so I didn't have a fire going."

"Wow, that's amazing," Victor said. "What were the chances of that happening?"

"I have a feeling that wasn't the end of it, though, Victor," Toby said as Marla vigorously agreed.

"What more?" Victor asked.

Toby nodded to Quade who aswered the question. "That wind was part of an electrical storm moving across the area right then. A bolt of lightning hit the steeple, shattering it into a lot of pieces - while the cross came straight down the chimney unharmed."

"Did you give that back to the people," Cindy asked.

"I did - and they made a new steeple, put it on top, and as far as I know its all there intact to this day."

Toby checked the time and said. "Now we should clean up this room from our newest arrivals."

* * *

The Gordons' master bedroom had been transformed into a kind of war room with a large map pinned to the wall by the vanity.

That in turn was cleared as a desk with a laptop computer on it beside a line of cell phones. Papers were scattered all around.

Dragenlyte wore a green visor and a maniacal expression as she scanned a smartphone, then consulted the computer monitor. "Okay, there's no sign of them in those two towns, they haven't bought gas with a credit card, and didn't fly out of any major airport."

She waved her hands to chase off annoying possibilities.

"If they're in cahoots with someone with a small plane there's no way I can check all the places they could take off and land so I'll refuse to believe the Jansen brat could have arranged something like that unless he'd been planning today as long as I have - and nobody plans farther ahead than I do. They all say it's too crazy."

She stepped to the large map with several concentric circles drawn on it with the city center at the middle. She marked two Xs close to one another in one quadrant with a black felt-tip marker. There were Xs all over, more concentrated in the inner circles.

She muttered to herself, "This is all rational. There's a limit to how far they could drive in that time and it helps that there are only so many roads. I should be getting close to knowing their exact location since I've called in every resource I have."

Klemper entered and said, "Mrs. Harbison is asking for you. She has people to introduce you to as she promised."

"Tell her I'm busy," Dragenlyte snapped without looking over.

"You are going to pass up a chance to meet people who might be useful to you in future? Then you vil dare try to blame me. Bad move."

Dragenlyte waved her away more emphatically.

Klemper laughed, "Der young ones are having more effect than they could have hoped. They vould dance with glee if they could hear and see you like dis."

"I will not be defied! They're going to do what I tell them to or... or something nasty might happen."

"Just the thing to let Mr. Noble hear you say," Klemper chided.

"Leave Austin out of this."

"But he is der big big part of vhat it is about. Meeting the friends of the Harbisons will be more useful in snaring him than anything you can achieve bringing the brats to heel."

"You're right. This will wait," Dragenlyte decided and marched over to precede Klemper out the door.

Klemper reached up and lifted the visor from her head as she passed saying, "I was fearing you needed a head shrinking doctor for sure."

Chapter 24

In the Quade living room, Marla and Victor helped Quade try to brush the foam pellets off the drapes, walls, and furniture with dust brushes and cloths. The work was slow and frustrating since the pellets clung to everything they touched..

Cindy was looking out the front window and called, "Hey look everybody, it's snowing hard now. It's like in a movie."

"They said on the radio that the storm could be major or it might only brush by us and it isn't certain yet which," Quade noted.

"Why won't this fake snow come off when we shake the drapes?" Victor asked as he brushed in frustration just as Toby and Febbraro entered from the kitchen with trash bags.

Toby answered, "Static electricity is why, Victor. Basic science."

"There must be a better way to do this," Marla grumbled. "I brush the pellets off and half of them stick on the brush and go back on the wall on my next swipe."

Febbraro said, "It should help when we get what's on the floor up so you can see how much new stuff you're getting onto the floor for the next sweep-up. At least it'll make your effort seem more successful."

Toby and Febbraro worked together to scoop the pellets from the bare wooden floor areas into trash bags.

"Isn't there a machine to do this?" Victor asked.

Everyone stopped to consider that question.

Quade said, "Actually there is. My shop vacuum. I'm so focused on the mess I made that you all have to help clean up that I'm not thinking enough about the easiest way to get the job done."

"We're all distracted by the weird stuff going on," Marla said.

Febbraro said, "I was gonna ask if that was in working condition and available, Fred.

"I'll be back in a few minutes. Don't waste energy on this in the meantime," Quade urged them and headed for the front door, picking up his coat from a chair as he went.

The others settled into seats where they would not flock themselves while waiting.

* * *

As Dragenlyte reentered the Gordon condo master bedroom with Klemper close behind she said, "I thought the Harbisons knew more important people than this lot. A waste of apple-polishing time."

"Sour polished up apples. Dos people could any of dem be useful to you at some time," Klemper insisted.

"That's why I was gracious even though I was disappointed."

"You need to practice hard und often on der sincerity looks. I had to tell some that you have une bad tummy ache to explain your grumpy expressions. I did not fool dem but distracted dem."

Dragenlyte was insulted. "I don't need any help..."

"Yes, you do. So you are velcome. Und don't forget this extra service I did for you when you make out my year-end bonus check."

"Darn those kids! I'm so frustrated by their defiance I can't think about anything except making them regret causing me trouble."

"Und Mr. Noble? If you can't think about him, you have lost it for whole und entire since they vere only important to you as part of your plot to win him."

"Thank you for trying to be the voice of good sense in the midst of turmoil, Olivia. Even if you don't succeed I appreciate the thought."

"Put that on a check to make it worth my while. Und remember dat I may go with der best offer for mine time. Und tell all."

* * *

Quade was soon back in the living room and had his heavy duty shop vacuum hose in hand, ready to go.

Febbraro stood close to the canister. Toby and the Gordons watched from across the room.

Quade said, "We should be ready to suck this stuff right off of everything."

"Please don't take it off the tree. It looks nice on there," Cindy said. "I've only see Christmas trees done like that in some stores, never before in anybody's house or apartment."

"It won't be a problem if it's already on there when we put the ornaments on although we will get some on us," Febbraro said.

"But we know how to get us vacuum cleaned," Vince said.

Quade said, "Okay. Let 'er rip."

Febbraro turned on the vacuum - and the canister's exhaust sent a cloud of foam pellets off the furniture and all over Toby and the three kids.

Febbraro flipped off the machine and hurried to help the newly flocked young people shake off as many of the pellets as they could right away. Quade stood staring in horror at what he had done.

"Next lesson. The vacuum has exhaust that can stir things up so we need to position it with that in mind," Toby said as he jumped up and down in place to see if that would shake off some of the pellets.

Then Marla pointed at her siblings and laughed. They returned the response.

Victor quickly worked himself up into a full-fledged giggle fest as he alternated between posing like a statue and shaking himself in as many ways as he could devise to unflock himself.

That had what was probably the deliberate intention of Marla and Victor – to reassure Mr. Quade that no serious harm was done or offense taken. Cindy just enjoyed it for the sake of having a new silly experience she would tell about for weeks to come.

Minutes later, Febbraro and Victor held the canister in place so it couldn't turn and thereby send the exhaust air in the wrong direction as Quade moved along vacuuming up the pellets.

Marla quipped, "I knew you had to be good for something, Vic. You're a natural as a vacuum exhaust direction guy."

He took a little bow in response.

Minutes later, the pellets were removed from hair, clothes, walls, furniture, and floor leaving only a light covering on the tree – which the group were preparing to decorate.

When the doorbell rang, Toby and the three Gordons exchanged worried looks.

Quade went to the front door to see who it was and soon led in the apologetic man who said, ""Hello. My name's Dennis Handerman."

Febbraro said, "Of course. You're looking for Heathcliff, right?"

"Yes. I don't want to bother people but I'm trying to locate him. Did you by chance see him?"

With a few honks the goose waddled into the room from the dining room. He now had a festive red ribbon tied around his neck and a small ornament taped on the back of his head.

Cindy said, "The cat's in the kitchen with the door closed so the big bird's being good."

Handerman wondered about that but opted not to ask.

"Is the goose's name Heathcliff?" Marla asked.

"I was warned and didn't intend him to be a pet but it sort of happened," Handerman replied with a little shrug.

"He escaped and flew away on you?" Febbraro asked.

This sounded interesting to the kids.

"It wasn't quite like that but I'm not certain what happened. My eyes were closed," Handerman admitted.

The others exchanged questioning looks about that.

"I'm glad to have him back though. I wasn't sure where he went," Handerman said as the goose waddled over to stand by him.

"He came down the chimney along with Mr. Quade and made the mattress explode," Cindy explained.

Now it was Handerman who had the questioning look, but since no one rushed to explain he went and picked up the goose saying, "Thank you for finding him. I hope he didn't cause too much trouble. I have to go do a special favor for someone so if you'll excuse me."

Everyone waved good-bye and Handerman left with his goose.

"Will that be Christmas dinner?" Toby asked.

"Not likely in my opinion," Febbraro answered. "A guest at Christmas dinner maybe, but not the entree."

"What's the entree?" Cindy asked Marla in a whisper.

"The food that's the center of attention. Uh, like the pot of stew or the fancy molded gelatin salad," her sister said.

When Marla looked over she got smiling thumbs-up gestures from Toby, Quade, and Febbraro.

*　*　*

In the condo's master bedroom Dragenlyte poured over her maps and notes. A cell phone rang. It takes her several rings and two false starts to determine which one it was.

"Good evening. Who is calling?"

"It's Austin, Sally. I'm still on the road out in the sticks and the storm's getting worse."

"Where are you? Perhaps I can have someone drive out and pick you up. I have a large car that stays on the road."

"That's not necessary, I'll be there for dinner tomorrow but I'll be later getting to the hotel than I expected tonight. I didn't want you to call them and get upset when I wasn't there yet."

"How considerate of you. Can't whoever is with you help with the driving?"

"Not possible since I'm traveling alone."

"Then perhaps you should cancel whatever stop you were going to make and continue right to the city," she suggested.

"When the dancing girls have prepared a special number in my honor? I don't think so. They might get frostbite if they don't keep warm dancing in the snow to please me."

"What does that mean?" She didn't succeed in making the words come out sounding amused and not suspicious and jealous.

"That you have no reason to be jealous. If I planned to stop to visit with a rival I'd never have told you anything about my plans."

"Of course you're not doing anything like that. That thought never entered my head. Where did you say you're calling from?"

"See you tomorrow. Have a merry Christmas Eve." He hung up.

She put the phone back down among the others as she asked herself, "Did he deliberately not tell me his location? I suppose that at least this way I have more time to put things back in the order I insist on before I face him."

She checked the text on the computer monitor, then turned back to the cell phones.

"Wait, I can have his call traced and find out where he is even if he doesn't think it's important that I know. But which phone did the call come in on? It won't help if they trace the last call on the wrong phone. This one? No, that one? I'm not sure. Who can I blame for this?"

*　*　*

Toby stood alone on the porch of the Quade house making a cell phone call, his coat buttoned up to his chin to stay warm.

"City morgue, used parts department," Pawling answered.

"Shane, good fellow, it's Toby again. Sorry to bother you but I'm worried."

"So solly. Me no speaky English."

"Please, please, please don't hang up. The peace of Christmas for a bunch of great kids depends on you."

"To speak to the superhero booking agent you must dial one-three hundred and a bunch of ones. This is a recording."

"See, this is exactly why I need you."

"What now?"

"I need a fake person to send a false signal. It's a natural job for a man of a zillion voices like yourself."

"This still involves her, doesn't it?"

"She's not really that bad. But she may have been told where we are and I want to convince her that that report was wrong."

"Just call and tell her then. No need for *moi* to be involved."

"Two, or maybe better even three, total strangers calling with messages that point in the same false direction will convince her and I'll owe you big big."

"Big big?"

"Yeah, I'm that desperate," Toby said.

"Tell me what you have in mind. No promises that I'll agree to it or won't chicken out after I say I'm in, but at least I'll hear you out."

"That's part of why I'm confident I can get you considered for a well-paying job you'll love and be good at."

"Okay, that's a reward I'd be happy to claim," Pawling said.

* * *

Dragenlyte stared at the large map spread on the bed as if she expected the answer she wanted to magically appear there.

The house phone rang. It took her three rings to realize it wasn't one of the several cell phones.

She picked up. "Yes?"

"Have kinky message for Dragon Person?" Pawling said using a strange and unidentifiable accent.

"Who is this? Are you being insulting?"

"That no you, I no tell where kiddos are."

"You may give me the information," she replied, desperate enough for any lead to control her tongue at least for now.

"East south east. Half one hundred." The call was disconnected.

Dragenlyte looked at the phone for a long moment wondering if there was anything else she could garner from those words, then hung up.

Then an idea registered. She stepped to the big map and circled an area in the East South East section of the biggest circle she had drawn on it as the possible location. "Probably useless information but it doesn't hurt to consider it," she said.

* * *

The urban street was a spot near a major intersection with a lot of foot and vehicular traffic. Pawling dropped coins in the pay phone near the corner and adjusted his hooded parka and stood facing the wall, head down, as he waited.

"Good evening. What do you want?" Dragenlyte asked.

"Singing telegram." He sang, "East is east and nothing's west, and the Gordon kids are there."

As a noisy bus pulled by, he held the handset out to let that sound drown his voice, then hung up. He hurried away.

* * *

Dragenlyte stood before the big map moving a closed marker lightly over the eastern section as she pondered.

Klemper entered and handed her another cell phone.

Dragenlyte said into the cell phone, "Yes?"

She listened, disconnected and handed that phone back to Klemper. Dragenlyte made a note on a pad of paper and started to gather all her materials together.

She directed, "Tell Mrs. Harbison we're leaving her in charge. She can have the doorman come up and lock up if we're not back when the party's over."

"Where are we going?"

"To follow up on a hot tip and surprise someone."

"I hate surprises," Klemper said making a sour expression.

"So will he, but too bad about that," Dragenlyte without smiling but still seeming to enjoy the prospect.

Chapter 25

Elaine Wurster, Quade, Toby, Cindy and Victor were busy but happy decorating the tree in the Quade living room. Quade handed ornaments up to Victor, who was proud to be the one on a ladder which made him important.

"I certainly didn't expect to be here doing this but it's fun," Wurster said. "Who'd believe I'm having fun because of nasty Sally."

"The lady herself would be most surprised and probably not pleased," Quade replied.

"She's not a total ogre but she does cause problems since you're not important, only what she wants is," Wurster said.

Cindy announced, "I'm ready again, Toby."

Toby lifted up the girl who had an ornament in each hand so she could place them higher on the tree, then put her down.

"I still vividly remember the first time I had a run in with Sally," Wurster said.

"How long ago was that?" Toby asked.

"Too many years to admit to," Wurster said.

"Nineteen years," Quade stage whispered with a laugh.

"My age," Toby said.

"I caught her stealing the town's things and the policeman on duty refused to stop her and her hired crew," Wurster said.

"Then when the rest of us learned what happened we decided there would be more troubles than it was worth to press charges when Elaine could tell us who was in charge of the operation," Quade said.

"From her car's license number. Backed up by her fingerprints from her car door if we needed further proof," Wurster said.

"But her face was a problem," Quade said.

The others waited for an explanation of that. When he realized that he said, "She was wearing a lot, I mean a lot, of makeup. Probably as a disguise, Elaine took pictures of her but even those of us who had met the stranger on the street knew the pictures made it hard to be sure it was her. So we side-stepped the troubles."

"What kind of trouble?" Victor asked.

"Expensive legal costs withouta strong likelihood we could win the case. Then the likelihood of her suing us when we didn't win. And the news attention from all of that that we didn't want," Quade said.

He stared at the floor for a moment as he debated with himself about saying more before, then said, "Earlier that evening, right in this room, she threatened to anonymously smear my Ramona if I caused her any trouble. I believed she could and would use any excuse to justify to herself doing that."

"I didn't know that until now," Wurster said quietly.

"I hated myself for not fighting her, but knew we had copies of the tubes made at the same time as backups for the old film in storage. I had those put up and pretended nothing had happened. Three of us put them in place the next night. Few even realized they were gone for a day. Their colors were brighter that the others and those who missed them that day probably thought they were being fixed," Quade said.

"I have no way to know who or how many people remember and resent her for that theft," Wurster said.

"I'm glad that you didn't keep trying to stir things up about the matter," Quade said.

"I guess I didn't really expect to find out, but since then as the Internet became a tool for me I've searched for hints of where the tubes went but found nothing about them," Wurster said

"Probably just as well if the town wouldn't do anything about them," Toby said. Quade nodded agreement.

Victor nodded that he got that - so Cindy nodded too.

"What would be the trouble if there was news attention? Don't all towns want some of that, Mr. Quade." Victor asked.

"Even back then, many of us were happier to have Festivity as mostly a bedroom community. Two other towns in the region had become tourist hot spots and changed in ways we still want to avoid. There's no easy or reliable way to control the effects of any news attention so we'd prefer to avoid it when we can," Quade said.

"At my own expense and without anybody else's approval or support, I went to the city hoping to confront her in a public place and embarrass, maybe even hurt her career, whatever it was, by telling the world what she did," Wurster said.

"At least what you claim she did. I immediately see a legal mess for you if you publicly accused her but didn't enough proof to convince a judge or jury," Toby said.

"A lawyer I talked to warned me about that. So I hoped to show up where she would see me and worry about what I was going to do to make her uneasy and therefore unhappy. Not nice of me, but I know she stole those things and shouldn't get away with it," Wurster said.

"Did you see her in the city?" Cindy asked.

"Several times. And I made sure she saw me. But after the first time, she'd go out of her way to avoid me. I still hope she was getting an ulcer worrying about what I was doing when I went to some trouble to get where she'd see me and have to change her plans to avoid letting me get close," Wurster said.

"Maybe worrying about what you had to say worried her more than how publicly you might accuse her of something," Toby said.

"And yes there is something I still want to tell her to spoil her satisfaction after as long as you've been around. I found something else when I was asking around about her visit. But I'll keep that to myself until I can tell her about it before an audience," Wurster said.

"We hope you won't get an easy chance to unload on her here today but we'll celebrate if you get and use the chance," Toby said.

"It's especially annoying the way she laughs at you when she's made a fool of you," Wurster noted.

"Or glares at you to try to scare you into doing what she wants," Quade said quietly.

"She deliberately encourages stories about how much of a witch she can be. I think that makes it easier for her to intimidate people into doing what she tells them to," Toby said.

Cindy chimed in with, "She's always nice to us when mommy or daddy are home. She's only mean and bossy if she's in charge of things."

"She usually knows when she can get away with stuff and when she'll get resistance. She hates it when she plans things and people won't go along," Toby said.

"Like you and the kids tonight," Quade suggested.

"Right. After this I'm off her Christmas gift list for sure," Toby replied.

"Does she give you a present, Toby? She doesn't get any for us," Victor noted.

Toby smiled as she said, "I'll bet she has something for each of you this year since you'd be expected to make a fuss and say thank you twenty times around her guests, Victor. I got a present once or twice when she wanted to use me like that for something, but not usually."

"Has she ever done anything good except to benefit herself in some way?" Wurster asked.

"Yeah, she has," Toby admitted. "She's a user but there are times when she has used her influence to help others in big ways. She often seems more unhappy and even desperate to succeed than mean."

Marla entered from the dining room with a bowl of popcorn. She put that on the sofa and looked out the front window. "It's not snowing as hard as before. Hey, there's a limousine up the street. I wonder where it's going."

Toby, Quade, and Wurster all froze for a moment, then Wurster and Toby rushed to the windows to look out.

Quade started that way, then realized he couldn't leave Victor alone on the ladder so he steadied that while the boy clambered down, then the two of them joined the others at the window.

"It couldn't be," Wurster said without conviction.

"I may have to go check on something," Quade whispered.

"It's not clear if it's coming here," Toby said. "It's going slow like the driver's looking for a street name sign."

"It's not coming here, it's turning up that other street," Marla said pointing out the window.

"Unless the driver hasn't found this address but is still looking," Toby said quietly.

"What would we do if it was Aunt Sally?" Victor asked. "Could we turn out all the lights and pretend we're not here?"

"If she's come this distance, she's not likely to be put off easily," Toby said with a shake of his head.

The others moved away and resumed decorating the tree. Only Victor stayed watching out the window.

"We could dress you kids in old people clothes and make your hair gray with powder and only let her look in through the window. She'd go away if there are no children here," Wurster suggested.

"We wouldn't have time since she'd be at the door before we knew we needed to disguise them," Toby pointed out.

"Hiding might work, disguises wouldn't," Quade said.

Marla said, "Maybe we could take Aunt Sally prisoner and lock her in one of the bedrooms until Christmas is over and she has no further plans for us."

"That doesn't sound like a nice thing to do on Christmas Eve," Cindy replied in a disapproving tone.

"Plus, I suspect she has plans for you three for longer than just tomorrow if she thinks you'll be useful," Toby said.

"I can solve the problem by having her arrested and taken away in handcuffs for the cheating she did twenty years ago," Wurster said, determined to neutralize with this threat.

"Twenty years is too long ago for the law to get involved unless she murdered somebody," Quade pointed out.

"Aunt Sally murdered somebody?" Cindy gasped.

"No, no, Cindy. Nothing like that," Toby hurried to clarify.

Febbraro entered from the dining room wearing an apron.

Marla said, "I just thought of locking her up but I knew right away that wouldn't be a fun thing for Christmas Eve. We need to focus on good stuff. Fun stuff."

"You're right, Marla. We've been worrying and letting things get mopey instead of enjoying the holiday," Toby said.

"Maybe we could all sing carols and she'd forget her other plans," Victor said.

"Or she'd call the police and have Toby arrested by saying he took us away without permission. Then the police would make us go with her," Marla said, unable to escape reality.

"But we'd say it wasn't true since it wasn't," Cindy insisted.

"But the police wouldn't try to sort it out tonight, they'd leave it to a judge some other day," Quade noted.

Wurster started to speak but then thought better of it.

Toby said, "Meanwhile we're focusing on having a good time and not worrying, remember?"

Febbraro said, "You're also probably pretty hungry by now so I have things cooking. We're limited by what you found left at the market but soon we can have a festive even if not lavish meal."

"John told me he knows kitchen magic," Cindy told the others.

Febbraro nodded agreement. "That is, I know a few tricks to make things a little fancier and to stretch limited quantities. I don't pull stewed rabbit out of a hat though."

Victor called from the window, "The limo's going up the hill where you can see the road far out there. It's going faster, like they know where they're going now."

"Which means it wasn't anybody we didn't want to see coming here so we can forget that possibility and relax," Toby urged.

"And string popcorn to put on the tree," Cindy said.

"If any's left we can put outside for the birds to eat," Marla said.

Toby asked, "Do you need help in the kitchen, John? Food's top priority."

Febbraro replied, "Things are cooking so I'm good until the rush to get it on the table. We could set the table though."

Toby whispered to Febbraro," Delicate question. Will there be enough for us to invite everybody to stay?"

He assured him, "We can feed an army. The more the merrier."

* * *

The limo drove on, the partition up so the driver didn't have to listen to the two women in the back. He was being paid at premium rate by the hour and had nothing better to do this evening than help them rack up a big bill.

He had insisted that Dragenlyte sign a credit card billing form before two witnesses before he would let them in the vehicle. Having been flown to the small local airport from the city by rented helicopter - and knowing the car rental agencies had closed by that hour (as if she would be seen driving any dinky rental car anyway) - she was stranded by her own doing and they all knew it.

When she prodded Klemper to snarl a threatening comment at the man, the price went up thirty percent. And Klemper laughed.

* * *

"The longer this takes, the longer I'll punish them - especially the oldest one."

"You were happy to send them away. They were happy to get away. It was der good solution for a time," Klemper said.

"But I insisted they be back in time to play the role I had planned for them. I wasn't giving them permission to make me look bad. I'm sure I was very emphatic about that," Dragenlyte said.

"Maybe in your head, but it didn't come from your mouth. A lot of other stuff did - but dat was all for der caterer and me."

"I pay you well to do what I tell you."

"At least you think so. But you be taking care. I have said many times. In a courtroom I remember what I heard and saw and don't pretend or say another line," Klemper said.

"It won't come to that. I'll find them and pay this man to drive the five of us back to the city. I'll deal with Toby another day. I have promises to important people to live up to," Dragenlyte said.

She looked up from her notebook where she had all the many details to be taken care of and out the window for the first time in a while. She used the limo's intercom to demand of the driver, "What is taking so long? Why aren't we there yet?"

"Where are we supposed to be? The last time you talked to me you admitted that you didn't see a landmark you thought would let you know where we were and told me to keep driving in circles until you spotted something you recognized."

"I'm sure I did not tell you to drive in circles," she snapped.

"Should we listen to the tape to be sure?" he asked.

Kempler was smiling and nodding that that was the directive the boss had given.

"I certainly never meant literally in circles."

"And I haven't been driving in them. I've been driving the local roads getting farther and farther from where you last said you didn't know where we were after giving me specific directions to get us there."

"I'm distracted and things look different in the dark and snow," Dragenlyte grumbled. She closed her phone and they drove on.

"You said back in der city dat you knew an address. Did you tell him to take us dere," Klemper asked.

"I thought I had it written down but I can't find it. But I was there once and I remember the house as being distinctive enough that I expect to recognize it. It's the cutesy town names that have me messed up. I tend to filter out anything cutesy."

"Dere is other obvious thing to do but you keep not doing it. That says something but mostly only you know vhat," Klemper said. Then she gasped as she realized it. "You forgot your book of the old addresses and dere is not me or any you can trust to find it and look up the name and address in it and tell you over the phone."

"It was clear to me at that airport that people knew me and seemed amused that I was there. I refuse to mention the name of the owner of the house and feed the local gossip chatter. If I could at least remember the town name I'd have this driver stop at a roadside pay phone and look up the address in the phone directory," Dragenlyte said.

Klemper pulled a folded state map from her handbag and tapped her boss on the nose with it, then reached up and turned on the inside dome light.

"You are like I have never seen you before with being upset and it is making you dumb, dumb, dumb," she said. When the boss started to object, Klemper said, "Look at the map. See der town names. See if one jumps up as familiar."

Dragenlyte gestured that she realized that was sensible but still was not inclined to do it.

Klempel waved that off and said, "Use your fancy phone to look for the name in the hanging in the air invisible phone book."

Even as Dragenlyte recognized that that was the easy and the obvious way to get them where she wanted to be, she resented her maid pointing it out. In fact having to point it out. Klemper made it a bit easier by turning to look out the window to ignore her now.

Dragenlyte tossed the paper map back in Klemper's lap, then checked the state map on her fancy phone.

Several town names were familiar. Google map let her search views of the town on her list until she found what she thought must be the place she wanted and got its address from that source.

She buzzed the driver and told him to take her there.

He asked if she was sure about that address. She said yes and to take her there post haste.

Twenty minutes later the limo sat near the rubble and ruins of a recently burned down house of the size and central fireplace that she remembered.

The driver said, "The fire last week was a big news story around here. Nobody was hurt but there's not much left. Is there any place else you want to check?"

"I have to check the map again. I got a message that they were settling in for the night so I think - I hope - there's another place."

"Tell who the visitors are vhat you vant to find," Klemper urged.

"No, I'm in charge so I'll handle this," Dragenlyte said.

"Der three Gordon children. You have heard about them?" Klemper asked the driver.

He looked at the women for a long moment as he considered how to answer that. What all had he been hearing on the local chatter places? Who might be hurt by him helping these two?

* * *

Marla helped Quade and Wurster set the dining room table.

Wurster said, "It's lucky you dropped in, Fred. They wouldn't have known where to find all these dishes on their own."

"They're very nice," Marla said admiring the pattern of a plate. "They make the food seem special because it's on something so pretty."

"My Ramona, God rest her, picked out the pattern. Back then we had big dinners with lots of folks so we needed stacks of everything."

"That explains the big table too," Wurster said with a nod. "Most dining room sets only have four chairs. And the table cloth's in good condition. It was stored nicely."

"It hasn't been used for a lot of years but it looks fine indeed," Quade agreed with a bit of pride.

* * *

Cindy, Victor, and Toby were hanging large holiday stockings made for the purpose with names on pieces of paper attached to them from the mantle in the living room.

"These are neat stockings to hang," Cindy said.

"We can get a lot of goodies in one of these," Victor agreed.

"Mr. Quade knows all that's stored here so it's lucky for us that he came by. I hope to get him a big reward for doing that," Toby said.

"I hope those people at the party at our house don't hurt our stockings," Cindy said with concern in her voice.

"I'm sure they'll enjoy them as part of the decor but won't touch them," Toby assured her. "They have their own at their homes."

"Now I need somebody to show me what you do to string the popcorn. Victor, do you know how?" Cindy asked.

"I haven't done it before but I saw people in a TV special about old time celebrations do it so I can figure it out," he said.

Those two sat on the sofa with a bowl of popcorn between them and Victor began to prepare needles and long threads. Cindy watched carefully, eager to learn.

"While you do that, let me see if I can't get a really great treat for you kids on Christmas Eve," Toby said. He put on his coat, made sure he had his cell phone, and went out on the porch.

Victor demonstrated as he instructed Cindy. "Easy enough but you have to pay attention. You push the needle through the corn but have to be careful not to crush it – or to stick yourself with the point. Then you slide it along the string like this."

Cindy whispered, "What's Toby's surprise going to be?"

Victor whispered back, "It won't be a surprise if we know."

But they got up and tiptoed over to peek out the front window at Toby, his back to the window, making a cell phone call.

"He's calling someone on his phone," Victor said.

"Probably telling Santa where we are," Cindy said, happy to know that was being taken care of.

Chapter 26

Wurster, Quade, and the three Gordons were stringing popcorn and decorating in the living room when Toby opened the front door as he called, "Come on it, we're happy to see you."

With the jangle of a set of sleigh bells, Bob Lapinski, tall, heavy set, and so happy to be here doing this that he could hardly keep from throwing up his arms and dancing, entered in a somewhat moth-eaten Santa costume that barely fit him. He toted a large cloth bag his mother had made for him by sewing up the sides of a sheet. There would turn out to be a variety of wrapped packages in it.

"Ho, ho, ho! Hi, everybody, it's me, Santa Claus. Straight from the North Pole. *Brrr*, it's cold up there."

The others smiled but no one was very enthused.

"I brought you presents since it's Christmas Eve and that's what Santa does on this night, right?"

Febbraro entered from the kitchen with Mrs. Lapinski, who was all smiles.

Bob left his bag near the entry and moved around the room shaking hands with each person. "Merry Christmas. Glad to see you. Bet you didn't expect to actually see Santa did you?"

The others smiled politely and shook his white-gloved hand.

He said, "The hope has come true. I have goodies to put in the stockings that are hung by the chimney with care."

He rummaged inside his bag as the others waited patiently.

Finally he extracted a plastic bag with a store name on it that containing small items and held it up saying, "Straight from the elf's workshop."

He went along and put small items like packs of batteries, boxes of raisins, and candy bars in each stocking.

Mrs. Lapinski said quietly to Febbraro, "This is so nice. He wanted to do this so much. He'll be happy for the whole year."

That done, Bob hesitated, looking from an empty chair to the people around the room, debating with himself how to do this.

Toby called, "Why don't we make this simple for you, Santa. You sit in that chair and hand us our presents when you call our names."

Bob hesitated about that. Mrs. Lapinski gestured to Toby that he needed to clarify that.

Toby got the silent message and said, "What I mean is I'll say the name and that person will come over to get a present from you. Will that work?"

Bob nodded and smiled and sat in that chair saying, "Ho, ho, ho. That's a good idea... uh."

"I'm Santa's helper Toby," Toby helped him by saying.

"Yes, of course," Bob agreed. Then he realized his bag was out of his reach and started to get up but Toby gestured for him to stay put.

Working together, Toby and Victor slid the bag full of packages over beside Bob in his chair.

"Ho, ho, ho. I say that a lot. Ho, ho, ho. Merry Christmas."

"Merry Christmas, Santa Claus," Cindy called.

Toby bent down by Bob and whispered, "It'll be easier if you let me know which person you want to come up next so I don't call the names in the wrong order."

"Ho, ho, ho." Then Bob whispered, "Okay. First the little girl."

Toby announced, "Santa's first present is for Cindy!"

Cindy smiled and went to Bob, who handed her a small wrapped package from his bag.

At that moment Wurster's cat came out from under the chair Bob was in and sniffed at his bag.

Bob was taken by surprise but delighted when Cindy gestured that she wanted to give him a hug before she moved away.

"Well ho, ho, ho, that's so nice," he said.

Cindy returned to her seat, placed the wrapped box on her lap, and waited to see who was next.

"Aren't you going to open it, Sweety?" Bob asked, not certain if there was a problem with what he was doing.

Thus prompted, Cindy carefully undid the wrapping and lifted out a package of three bars of facial soap.

Bob whispered to Toby, "I hope that's all right. I didn't have time to go shopping."

Cindy said, "Thank you, Santa. This smells nice and I like being clean."

Bob beamed happily.

Beside him, the cat nosed a bit deeper into his bag, climbing up on the side of it. When he reached for the next package he bumped the bag with his foot – and the cat fell inside.

" Now I have something special for that fine young lad uh…"

"Victor Gordon, come on over. You're a winner!" Toby called.

"Yes, Victor. That's the one," Bob said as he reached into the bag without looking, lifted out the cat by it nape, and smiled as he held it out to Victor who had come over to him.

Victor stared at the cat in Bob's hand and his questioning look prompted Bob to really look at what he was holding.

Startled, he dropped the cat - which dashed into the dining room while Bob did a goldfish-breathing imitation in surprise.

Victor wanted to laugh, but only smiled to not embarrass him.

"Sorry, Santa, you didn't bring that with you. It's just a curious inspector checking your bag," Toby said. "What did you bring Victor?"

Careful to look this time, Bob took a foot-square box, shook it to verify its contents, then handed it to Victor.

Off to the side Febbraro leaned close and whispered to Toby, who nodded and smiled.

Victor's face registered his disappointment that the box was so light but then he caught himself and smiled blandly.

Victor sat on the floor and opened the present - lifting out a billed cap with John Deere Tractors printed on it. He plunked it on his head - where it slipped down and covered him from his nose up.

Toby said, "One size fits all when you snap the thingee in the hole in back." He lifted the hat off Victor, adjusted the back, and returned it to the boy's head.

"That makes you an official country boy," Quade told Victor.

Victor said, "Thanks, Santa. It's just what I wanted but didn't expect to get."

Bob beamed and everyone else smiled tolerantly. He said, "Now for the other young person."

"Marla, that would be you," Toby said.

Bob looked startled when Marla stepped forward. He gestured for Toby to bend down for a conference. He whispered, "I thought there were two boys."

Toby whispered back, "Give her whatever you brought and she'll take it graciously."

Bob said, "Also I didn't know these others would be here. I only have empty boxes..."

"It'll be okay, Santa," Toby assured him. "Hand them out and I'll give them the signal not to open them."

Bob smiled weakly and handed a box to Marla saying, "Ho, ho, ho. Merry Christmas."

"Thank you, Santa." Marla curtsied and took the package back to her seat.

She opened it and held up a boxed set of screw drivers.

"Practical gifts for everyone. Very smart, Santa. Santa will give the rest of us our presents in a bit but there's supposed to be a big surprise delivered by some of his other helpers right about now," Toby said.

He smiled as the doorbell rang right on cue. He said, "We should all go answer this."

Everyone, including Santa Bob, gathered in the entry.

Toby pulled open the door - to find Dragenlyte and Klemper standing there.

Dragenlyte said, "Surprise. Happy moment for all. I'm here to rescue you."

Chapter 27

Quade, Wurster, and Victor gave *Home Alone* hands-on-cheeks silent screams and ran into the kitchen.

Cindy and Marla took hands, walked in and flopped on the sofa looking unhappy.

Toby just stood and stared at the new arrivals.

Febbraro looked at them as if assessing what species they were.

Bob looked around in frightened confusion. After a whispered conference with Febbraro, Mrs. Lapinski led Bob by the hand into the dining room. Bob asked in a whisper, "Who is she?"

His mother answered, "Apparently an infamous Dragon Lady."

Toby finally said, "Aunt Sally. Fancy meeting you here."

"I'll deal with you later, Toby Jansen. First I have to be sure the poor dears are all right," Dragenlyte said sharply.

Suddenly Toby snapped alert as an idea hit him.

He quickly closed the door before Dragenlyte could enter saying, "Thanks for stopping by, but we have a full house already."

Dragenlyte shouted, "Open this door this minute, Toby."

Toby looked for some way to do what he needed to. Febbraro nodded that he could hold the door. Toby nodded agreement.

Toby called to the two women on the porch, "Since I'm renting this house tonight I get to say who's welcome and you were not invited to our party."

Febbraro replaced Toby at holding the door almost closed while Toby hurried into the living room to his backpack.

"Olivia, get us inside," Dragenlyte shouted, then stepped aside to watch this with amusement.

Klemper revved herself up, then rushed at the door to throw her shoulder against it.

At the last second, the door opened, Febbraro stepped out into position and grabbed the oncoming Klemper. He whirled her around a hundred and eighty degrees and released her. She narrowly missed Dragenlyte, then her momentum carried her to the side railing of the porch - where she pitched over that head first and out of sight.

"You're not welcome to come in means you don't come in," Toby repeated. He completely closed the door while Dragenlyte stared at him in a mixture of awe and fury.

She never even looked to see if Klemper was all right.

Klemper came charging around the side of the porch and up the steps, leaves sticking to her clothes and hair.

She prepared for another assault on the door.

Febbraro opened the door and waved them in.

"Toby says you can come in now."

Toby, the three Gordons, and Febbraro were all in the living room. Bob and Mrs. Lapinski sat at the table in the dining room but where they could see most of the living room. The others were not in sight. Toby stood by the decorated tree holding a video camera.

Dragenlyte entered dramatically, shrugged off her fur coat and held it out for Febbraro to take. She released it, but he didn't move so it fell to the floor.

To Dragenlyte's added annoyance he then kicked the expensive coat out of the way without a word and hardly even looking at it.

Klemper hung back in the entry, keeping her options open in case she needed to move to a particular spot in a hurry.

"I've come to take the children home. That's all that needs to be said," Dragenlyte announced.

"Do you want to go with her, Kids?" Toby asked.

In unison Marla, Victor, and Cindy answered, "No, we want to stay here."

"Children don't get to decide these things. I'm in charge and I say what happens," Dragenlyte said with a snarl.

"Because their parents are lost in Eastern Europe and out of contact, isn't that what you told them?" Toby asked.

In unison Marla, Victor, and Cindy said, "Yes, that's what she told us."

Dragenlyte snapped her fingers, "Get your coats we're leaving now. No more dramatics."

"Be careful mit what you say, he has der recording machine," Klemper cautioned her quietly.

"This was a Christmas present to myself and a great choice. It lets me tape what's said and done so that it's not just my word against yours," Toby said.

"That silly thing doesn't scare me," Dragenlyte said and gestured for Klemper to take the videocam.

Klemper started across the room toward Toby, but Febbraro stepped in to block her path. Toby kept taping everything.

Klemper feigned to one side but Febbraro didn't move, only stared straight at her with a look that said he would stop her anyway she tried to get around him.

Klemper sneered at him and walked straight at him, expecting him to give way.

Febbraro grabbed Klemper, turned her around, force marched her into the entry, shoved her into the coat closet and closed the door on her. Then he casually leaned against the door assuring that she wouldn't get out until he allowed it.

He commented, "What a waste. It's Christmas Eve and all these two can think about is how to use other people. It's sad."

"Spare us all the holiday spirit talk that nobody really means," Dragenlyte said with a sneer.

"I mean it," Febbraro said. "I'm having the best Christmas Eve in years because I said no to those who wanted to use me, not just share with me."

Dragenlyte guffawed, "Next thing you'll tell me the real Santa Claus and not that sorry substitute in the other room is going to drop by and leave you all presents."

"Only those who have been good get presents. That's the rule," Cindy noted.

"But the man in the red suit in the dining room is an example of what it's about," Toby said. "He's having a good experience doing his part to make the fun happen and we're all going along with it because that's what makes it fun."

"Humbug. You're wasting your time and you're wasting mine," Dragenlyte replied. "The children are coming with me and right now. Put that silly camera away, Toby."

"Santa wanted me to have it so I figure I'm meant to use it," he said. "We're about ready to have dinner so we're not going anywhere tonight. But we'll wave goodbye and promise to see you after Christmas if you want."

Dragenlyte made an ugly face and said, "I am so sick of hearing Santa Claus nonsense! I'll make you a deal. If the real Santa Claus shows up here tonight I'll do nothing but nice things for three months. But if he doesn't show - leaving clear evidence of his presence - you deliver the children by lunch tomorrow."

"I can't speak for them," Toby replied without hesitation.

Cindy said, "I agree to the deal. Santa will be here, you'll see."

"We won't have a real choice anyway," Marla said in a resigned tone.

Victor shrugged his agreement.

"Okay, we accept your deal," Toby said. "We have it all on video in case anyone needs to be reminded of the terms."

At that moment the doorbell rang.

Chapter 28

Febbraro opened the door and found well-dressed and handsome Austin Noble standing there.

Febbraro said, " I was expecting somebody else. Can I help you?"

"I'm not sure if I have the right address. I'm looking for Toby Jansen."

"For what? What's he done?"

"Pulled a fast one from what he said. Also invited me to visit."

Toby called from the living room, "Is that the surprise you told me about, John?"

Febbraro called back, "No, it's a guy looking for you. Says you're expecting him."

Toby hurried out, still with the video camera in hand. Noble was still on the porch.

Toby said, "Are you..? Yes, you are." He whispered, to the new guest, "She showed up here. She's inside right now. Maybe you don't want to come in after all."

Dragenlyte came to the doorway and demanded, "What's going on now? Send the intruder away and close the door."

"Good evening, Sally," Noble said.

"Austin! What are you doing here?"

Noble stepped inside and closed the door. He took off his coat and Febbraro took it from him.

"I was in the neighborhood and decided to stop in and meet your nephews and nieces. Why are you way out here?"

"I... I was worried sick when they drove out this way and I didn't think they could make it back to the city because of the storm."

Febbraro opened the coat closet door. Klemper was curled up, asleep on the floor. He hung up Noble's coat and left the door ajar.

Noble caught a glimpse of a person on the floor and looked his questions at Febbraro who said, "It's a long story, but she's only worn out from jousting at windmills."

The kids were on the sofa. Toby stayed behind it and continued to tape with the video camera.

Dragenlyte sat in one chair, Noble in another. Febbraro went to the kitchen. Bob and Mrs. Lapinski moved to where they could see those in the living room.

Wurster and Quade stayed out of sight.

"I'm sorry you found me in this state, Austin," Dragenlyte said with a dramatic sigh. "I've been frantic with worry for hours since I didn't know if the children were all right."

"They seem fine to me. It looks to me like young mister Jansen took good care of them," he said.

"Yes, but there was a breakdown in communication and I didn't know where they were or I'd have made sure they were in no danger."

"How was the party at their place? Did as many people who might be important to you show up as you expected?" Noble asked.

At that moment a bedraggled Klemper appeared at the doorway and said, "She stuck her nose up at them."

"It's more than about time you stopped napping on the job, Olivia," Dragenlyte snapped, then got up and moved to the sofa.

The children cringed away from her.

Then Victor got up and moved over to sit on a cushion in the fireplace. Cindy quickly followed suit.

This did not please the Dragon Lady who had to fight hard not to let her annoyance show too much.

"I'm sorry to hear that you didn't get the group you hoped for," Noble told Dragenlyte. "Perhaps at some other holiday function you'll meet the important ones."

"Of course since I'm the one responsible for the children while their parents are away on business, I won't have nearly as much time for socializing as usual," she continued in a half-whine.

"It's gracious and good of you to accept the responsibility for supervising them. They must be a handful," he said.

"But I always insist that nothing's too good for the children. Their happiness must be my top priority," Dragenlyte insisted in true domestic martyr mode.

"Didn't their parents arrange for Mrs. Norton to stay with them as they usually do when they go away?" Toby asked, knowing and intending to take this talk where the lady would not want it to go.

"It seems she wasn't available so I jumped in to save the day," Dragenlyte replied. "It also gives me a chance to bond with the dears and nurture them. I don't have nearly enough chances to be around young people even though I adore it when I'm with them."

"I knew you were looking forward to introducing me to them tomorrow night so when I learned they were here I decided to get out of the snow and see what's so special about them," Noble said looking over the brood.

Dragenlyte moved toward Marla saying, "Being around them I just want to hug them all the time,.

The girl flinched away, then got up to straighten a decoration and remained standing well away from the sofa.

Toby moved around to where he had an unobstructed view of Dragenlyte with the video camera and focused on her which made her slightly more than a bit self-conscious but she resisted complaining.

"There is two important things you can do to make the kids happier, Aunt Sally. Simple enough things really," Toby said.

"Well why are you holding back, Toby dear? Tell me what they are," Dragenlyte said, straining to sound enthused.

Marla gave the answer. "First, tell us where mom and dad are."

Noble was startled to hear this. "They don't know where they're parents are on Christmas Eve?"

"There was talk about them being lost somewhere in Eastern Europe and possibly never making it home. Needless to say that has them quite worried," Toby explained.

Dragenlyte made a bold attempt at making light of the whole matter. "Did it come out that way? How terrible. Olivia should have said that they're on a diplomatic mission and knew they wouldn't make it home for the holiday. I'm sure the State Department knows where they are."

"So they're not lost and in danger?" Toby asked to clarify this.

"Not as far as I know. I doubt that I ever said anything that should have been interpreted to mean that," Dragenlyte insisted. "But we need to focus on the welfare of the children, not any silly past misunderstandings. I assure you, Austin, I'm doing all I can to keep them safe and secure."

"Have you talked to their parents today, Aunt Sally?" Toby asked, not about to let her off the hook so easily.

"I certainly haven't been to Eastern Europe, no," Dragenlyte said with a gesture to convey how silly that and all these questions were.

"Have they called you on the phone?" Victor asked, sensing where this might be leading.

"I've been very busy for days now. I can hardly be expected to remember each phone call I've received," she replied.

"Do you have a problem with your memory?" Noble asked.

That set off the alarm bells in her head so Dragenlyte almost shouted, "No, of course not. I'm fit as can be. Oh, I remember now, they did call. I'm to wish the children a happy Christmas from them."

"What time did they call? Where did they call from?" Marla was looking around to see if anyone else found this shocking.

"Unimportant details, dear. I gave you the important message," Dragenlyte said and looked around for something she could redirect everyone's attention to.

"I would sure want to know the details if I were them and just learned that my parents weren't as lost as what I was told a few hours ago implied," Toby persisted.

Before Dragenlyte could make additional dismissive comments Noble said gravely, "So would I."

"They called about six o'clock this evening. I said the children were out for a walk to look at the light displays and I wasn't sure what time they'd be back in, but that all was fine."

"Did they say they'd call back later?" Noble asked.

"Perhaps they did, I'm not certain. I handed the phone to Olivia so I could handle details with the caterer."

Klemper shrugged, "I didn't know who it was and thought the call was over so I disconnected."

Toby said, "Before we forget it in all the questions that raises. The second thing you can do is agree here before us all that any money you claim is owed to you by anyone or everyone who lives in this town you are freely giving to the owner of this house as rent on this truly fascinating place that gave the kids a shelter out of the snow today."

He gestured around the room. "Do the young Gordans agree with me that this house has been a fine shelter and worth that price?"

The three kids nodded emphatic agreement.

Dragenlyte wondered what that meant, then looked around the room and understood as Fred Quade and Wurster stepped into view from where they had been staying out of sight in the dining room.

She was stunned. Had the Jansen brat planned this whole thing to tweak her by undoing her years-long manipulation? Did he think she wouldn't see what he was doing and turn that idea down flat?

"And for good measure, you agree that any of the cash you gave me to cover our expenses while I got the kids out of your way that I have left at this point is mine to keep for my trouble even though we had not formally agreed to that until now," Toby said.

She began to sneer and give this troublemaker whom she had been hassling whenever she could for years a verbal response no one present would forget for a long time.

Then Noble leaned over to be sure she saw him to remind her he was there and listening too.

It took her a great effort not only to say it but to do so without choking on the words. "I agree. I'm paying the rent on this house. No one from this town owes me anything from today."

"Owes you any money, at least. Memories don't wipe off the mental books as easily," Tody said quietly but everyone heard and most nodded agreement.

"I want to clear your reputation on this," Wurster said. "After your previous visit, I checked out what you looked at in the Festivity Historical Society files. Dear old Mrs. Doorwatche, may she rest in peace, was helpful to a degree but not fully attentive overall. She did, however, always carefully log all requests, including yours, for the microfiche files of the town records."

Dragenlyte tried to wave this aside. "So what?"

"Her log listed you being given and the reader machine showed you looked at several that were never returned. She made a note about that but then got sick so no one followed up in it."

"She was helpful to a degree but too chatty for my taste."

"Now the Society plans an investigation of that since some of the old documents about the donation of items from a silent movie were on them but the originals have been lost. For the record, did you remove any of those files?"

Dragenlyte's hesitation registered as significant to most in the room. Finally, she sked, "Why would I do that? That's a dumb question and you're spoiling our party."

Wurther said, in a *since you asked* tone, "Of course I can only speculate on your motive then or when you removed other town property without authorization. Maybe you wanted more time to check the records for other things to steal."

Noble noted the lack of surprised looks around the room.

"That's outrageous! I defy you to prove any material I was given access is gone forever," Dragenlyte said with a tiny grin.

"So everyone can rest easy about this, when I reported the losses the microfiche pages were replaced from duplicates of every-thing stored in another building in town," Wurster said.

"Which I seem to remember reading back at about that time burned down, destroying everything inside," Dragenlyte said with a slight smirk.

"True - and interesting that you know that. The point is that when that happened copies of everything were back in the Historic Society building so they could be and were duplicated and stored in another place. Thus back to double security for contemporary investigations and historic studies," Wurster said.

"Perhaps you read about it in something that Betsy Brightly woman who was here at that time," Quade said.

Time to short-circuit this. Dragenlyte said, "I remember now. I discovered later that I had done so by accident as I hurried to get out of that stuffy office. I'm sure I soon mailed them."

"If so, they never made it back. But that tells us where they went at the time. I'm satisfied and with that," Wurster said.

Then that remarkable doorbell rang again.

Dragenlyte whispered to herself, "Thanks be, a distraction."

The others waited with interest as Febbraro went to the door.

He checked who was there, then smiled as he gestured to Toby that the expected surprise was here.

Toby announced, "Ladies and Gentlemen, may I present one of Santa's helpers with the pleasant surprise you were promised."

Febbraro pulled open the door and Handerman, wearing oven mitts, entered carrying a large roasting pan.

When everyone could see, Febbraro lifted the lid to reveal a large roasted turkey saying, "Dinner is served in ten minutes since all the rest is done in the kitchen."

Cindy asked timidly, "Mr. Handerman, is that...?"

"It's not Heathcliff, he's in his pen at home having a big helping of his favorite food. This isn't a goose and it's nobody that I knew," Handerman assured her.

"Smells good!" Victor declared.

"Everyone is invited to help us enjoy it since I'm assured we have plenty of food," Toby said.

"What about the Christmas tree?" Cindy asked.

Victor looked at her as if she had sprouted two extra heads and said, "Trees don't eat birds."

"No, I mean should we finish decorating it before we eat?" Cindy explained patiently to him.

"I think from the hungry looks around the room that feeding our faces comes first. The tree will still be here when we've refueled ourselves," Toby suggested.

"I want the wishbone!" Victor called out.

"First one to call it gets it was always the rule in my family," Febbraro said with a happy shrug.

"I suppose that since I'm invited I should at least sit at the table to be polite," Dragenlyte said demurely.

"Watch her eat more than any of the men. I've seen it lots of times," Klemper said without making a big deal of it.

Chapter 29

Ten minutes later several additional chairs were in use around the large dining room table. Toby sat between the three Gordons and Dragenlyte. Noble was between her and Klemper. Mrs. Lapinski, Bob Lapinski (without the Santa beard), and Wurster were also here.

Febbraro stood at one end, ready to carve the turkey. Dishes of potatoes, vegetables, and the other fixings were on the table.

Quade fussed with a boombox on a side table then said, "It was a tradition in this house for many years to start Christmas Eve dinner with this instead of the usual grace. Think your own good thoughts."

He pushed a button and a vocal version of *Bless This House O Lord We Pray* began to play. All except Dragenlyte bowed his or her head. She looked around at that and finally bowed hers too.

When that finished, Quade turned off the music and sat down saying, "Now enjoy the meal, a gift from a whole bunch of people here in the town of Festivity."

"Merry Christmas to us all," Cindy called cheerily.

"And to all a good share of dessert," Victor added.

That evoked laughs all around and everyone pitched in to pass the food around and enjoy it.

Noting that Dragenlyte put almost nothing on her plate, Noble gave her an comical sucked-in-cheeks gaunt look.

She whispered to him, "What is that supposed to mean?"

"That I worry about women who won't eat a hardy meal. I think you can be too thin and I'm not turned on by the thin as a reed look."

So Dragenlyte filled her plate, hoping her relief at enjoying this food wasn't too evident. Noble nodded his approval.

Toby said to Quade, "Thank you, Fred. That was a wonderful way to start the meal and the holiday."

"My wife started us doing it - but after she was gone it didn't seem right. Tonight it feels right again."

Noble said to Dragenlyte, "This is like being a Norman Rockwell character. It's a new experience for me. We didn't have much family togetherness when I was growing up."

"I'll deny it if you ever bring it up later, but I'm enjoying this much more than I would a fancy dinner with movers and shakers. But I can't answer the bottom line question," she said.

"What's that?" he asked.

"How will this help my career?"

"It broadens your horizons and makes you more fully a person."

"Do I need that?"

Noble said, "I can't speak for you, but I can certainly use some stretching out and this seems like a pleasant and painless way to experience another slice of society."

"It's surely different from what I've known 'til now," Sally said.

* * *

The buzz of conversations and laughter from the dining room continued as Santa Claus smoothly descended the chimney into the fireplace and stepped into the living room with his bag full of presents. He looked around and smiled.

Santa gestured at the half-decorated tree and suddenly it was finished and breath-taking.

He tapped each stocking on the mantle and it suddenly brimmed with goodies.

The cat stepped out and mewed a quiet greeting. Santa nodded and it had a ribbon tied loosely around its neck, bow at the back.

And a catnip mouse to play with.

He emptied his bag and a stack of wrapped packages slid right over and under the tree on their own.

He stepped back into the fireplace, and laying his finger aside of his nose, and giving a nod, up the chimney he rose.

* * *

The sound of sleigh bells momentarily mixed with the voices in the dining room. First one, then another stopped talking to listen to the pleasant noises that sounded like they were directly overhead.

Cindy slipped from her chair and dashed into the living room.

The others resumed eating, although no one spoke while they waited for Cindy to return and report.

When she didn't come right back, Marla went to check on her.

When neither girl returned promptly, Victor went to check.

Victor was not a notorious quiet type. He shouted, "Oh wow! Out of sight! It happened. He's been here while we're still awake."

Toby, Febbraro, Quade, Wurster, Mrs. Lapinski and her son Bob went to see what was happening.

Dragenlyte and Noble exchanged looks but opted to stay put. Klemper didn't move, just hummed to herself, lost in her own world.

There were murmurs of wonderment from the other room.

Cindy entered and said, "You should come see this, Aunt Sally."

Toby came to the doorway and added, "You're not likely to take our word for this, you need to see it for yourself."

"But I'm not finished my dinner. Can't it wait?" Dragenlyte said.

"It can, but then you'll be the last to know and we all know you hate that," Toby said and went back into the living room.

Dragenlyte shook Klemper out of her dream state ordering her, "Olivia, see what's going on, I'm busy entertaining Austin."

Klemper shrugged and followed Cindy into the other room.

Seconds passed. Klemper didn't return or call back a report.

By now Noble was getting itchy, but Dragenlyte refused to show she had any curiosity about things.

Everyone else except Klemper all beamed with delight as they came back in to hurry and finish their dinner.

They glanced at Noble and Dragenlyte and either giggled or gave them pitying looks, but no one said anything.

Noble stood, saying, "I give in. I have to see what this is about. They came back to finish eating so I can too, my curiosity satisfied."

Dragenlyte stood to accompany him but made sure she showed no enthusiasm for whatever was happening.

When Dragenlyte entered the living room she focused fully on Klemper who was sprawled in a chair staring open-mouthed and at first Sally didn't look around to see the tree and the pile of gifts.

Noble saw everything right away. "Now that is truly magic!"

When Dragenlyte finally looked around, she literally jumped in surprise. "Where did all that come from?"

"At risk of sounding unscientific, I'd say the North Pole by way of a sleigh pulled by flying reindeer," Noble answered.

"That's not possible," Dragenlyte said.

"But you can see mit your own eyes dat the not possible can and does happen on Christmas Eve," Klemper said.

"Surely someone must have come in while we were busy eating and done this," Dragenlyte said, determined to stick with the strictly rational positions.

"Somebody did. The Santa person," Klemper agreed.

"He came down the chimney which is why we didn't feel a draft from the front door opening," Noble suggested.

"I suppose if you want to play along with them I can't stop you," Dragenlyte persisted in her doubts.

"I can't see any other explanation for this. Look at that, even the skittish cat got the treatment and its owner was at the table with us the whole time," Noble pointed out as he turned to go to the dining room.

"What are you going to do?" Dragenlyte asked him.

"Finish my dinner so I can be here when everyone opens those presents. I want to see what Santa brought everybody. Coming?"

She hesitated, shrugged, and followed him into the dining room. Klemper got up and followed them.

* * *

Soon, the twelve people who were at dinner were in the living room, some sitting on dining room chairs.

The kids and Toby sat on the floor near the tree to pass around the presents. Each child has an opened present beside him or her.

Bob Lapinski was opening his gift.

"You guys made out really well," Toby said to the kids.

"Santa brought us just what we wanted," Cindy said.

"He has a knack for that," Toby agreed.

Bob Lapinski held up a new Santa outfit and fake beard. "This is what I wanted more than anything. So I could do a better job of making the children happy. But I didn't tell anybody about it."

Cindy told him, "Santa knows. It's part of his job to know what we really, truly want."

Toby checked the tag on a gift and carried it to Klemper who sat almost hidden at the back of the group. "You're next, Ms. Klemper."

Klemper was excited but also embarrassed. "I did not expect a gift from anyone here. I'm afraid this is a mistake."

"It's from Santa," Cindy said. "He thinks about us all."

"Open it and see what it is," Dragenlyte said, more than a little curious about it herself.

Klemper tore off the paper, opened the box and stared in awed disbelief at its contents.

"Is it something insulting?" Dragenlyte asked.

Klemper held up a sweater. "It's beautiful. And so soft. I didn't dare hope I could have one of these when I saw dem in a store. Thank you, Mr. Santa Claus."

Minutes later, Quade, Wurster and Febbraro now also had opened gifts in their laps or beside them. Marla handed Toby a box saying, "This one has your name on it, Toby."

Toby shook it gently, listening. "The rattle doesn't tell me anything. I wonder what it could be?"

"Come on, open it. Don't keep us in suspenders," Victor urged, then guffawed at his own word play.

Toby stripped the paper off the box and opened it. He looked at the contents and laughed.

He held up a sweatshirt with *Superhero* printed on the front and back. "Santa has a sense of humor. I don't remember actually wishing for anything like this but from now on I have a superhero sweatshirt to wear when I set out to take on challenges."

"Santa obviously reads minds and knows our secret fantasies," Noble said with a laugh. "We won't know when you're wearing that under a coat except by your latest heroic actions."

Toby checked the tag on the last package, a small one, then handed it to Cindy who carried it to Dragenlyte.

"Santa left this one for you, Aunt Sally. Merry Christmas."

Dragenlyte took the gift with a weak smile but hesitated about opening it in front of everyone.

"I should wait until Christmas afternoon before I open my gifts. Who else is waiting for one?" she said.

"Yours is the last one," Toby said.

"No fair keeping us all in suspense," Noble said pleasantly but with a note of firmness in his tone. "Open it so we can all share the experience with you. Sharing the surprise is part of what Christmas gifts are about."

She whispered to him, "I'm afraid it might be a lump of coal."

He laughed, then realized she wasn't smiling. "My gosh, you're serious."

He took the box and hefted and squeezed it a bit. "Trust Santa Claus. He wouldn't play a dirty trick on you. He might leave nothing to teach you a lesson, but not a bad gift to humiliate you."

He unwrapped it and held the small box that was inside to her.

Reluctantly Dragenlyte opened that box and stared, wordless, at a small bottle of perfume in it.

"Is that bad? Something cheap and nasty?" Noble asked, still worried by her reaction.

"It's like the first bottle of perfume I ever owned," she said in awe. "They don't make it anymore, not that I'd wear it these days. It's out of fashion. But I've thought about how happy it made me when I received that first bottle."

"That Santa Claus guy does know us pretty well." Noble said. "I wonder if there's some special meaning to this?"

That made everyone interested in that question. Dragenlyte looked across at Toby who was looking at her and smiling pleasantly.

"It's evidence that the real Santa Claus was here. Only he would know about the meaning of this to me and be able to find this long gone brand," she said quietly.

"Was he for real, Aunt Sally?" Toby asked.

"Yes, Santa Claus really and truly by some magic did visit here tonight," Dragenlyte conceded.

That brought knowing smiles to all the others - except Noble who wondered what those looks meant.

"We'll be looking forward to the consequences of you accepting that," was all Toby needed to say.

Noble said, "Will somebody please tell me what that means. I'm obviously the only person not in on some secret."

"We'll let Aunt Sally explain it to you in her own way," Toby said.

Then he moved everyone along to other thoughts by saying, "Mrs. Lipinski baked those delicious pies pies for dessert and it's a shame to have what's left of them for the moment sitting there getting stale. Who wants some more?"

Chapter 30

All heads turned when a chorus of voices outside broke into a rousing rendition of the carol *Angels We Have Heard On High.*

The kids were at the window in a flash, Febbraro close behind them. He pulled back the drapes and raised the shade to let everyone inside have a view of the dozen local carolers.

"This is so great. Like all the storybook versions of Christmas," Marla said.

"Can we go outside to see them, Toby?" Cindy asked.

"Ask Aunt Sally since she's your legally designated guardian at the moment," Toby replied.

Cindy's face reflected her reluctance about this.

Dragenlyte said, "Of course you can put on your coats and go out on the porch."

"Can we go with them?" Victor asked. "That'd be the best fun."

"Go with them?" Dragenlyte wasn't sure she followed that.

"Go caroling at other houses," Marla said. "We know a bunch of carols by heart so we can sign along."

Dragenlyte hesitated about that. The other adults had already grabbed their coats and were ready to go outside.

"I think it sounds like a great idea," Noble said. "In fact if this group hadn't come along already tuned up and singing, I might have suggested it myself."

"Are you certain it's all right?" Dragenlyte worried.

"They'll be with a group who are going out of their way to make this a special time for them. They can't help but have a good time," he assured her.

"Then you may indeed go caroling if you wish, children. But don't sing off key or throw snow around."

"Oh heck, if you can only sing off key then do so but quietly. And if you can resist the temptation to toss a snowball or two you're more disciplined than I am," Noble said.

"Are you defying me?" Dragenlyte asked, not sure whether this was a matter she should take seriously.

"No, I'm trying to loosen you up," he responded. "It's pretty clear to me that you need that."

* * *

Out on the porch Toby checked his watch, then he stepped to intercept the kids as they came out of the house with their coats on. Quade, Wurster, and both Lapinskis had joined the carolers who were now into a rendition of *We Three Kings Of Orient Are*.

Febbraro stayed on the porch, happily watching the others.

"We're gonna go caroling with the group, Toby. Wanna come?" Cindy said, all excited.

"I'm gonna suggest you stay behind for just a few minutes since there's a special surprise just for you three due any minute," Toby said.

"But we'll miss the carol singing," Victor said in a tone that he hated because it sounded even to him like a whine.

"This won't take long. You'll be able to catch up and I'm betting that you'll enjoy it more then," Toby said.

"Can't it wait? I've never been able to go caroling before," Victor said, hardly able to stand still he was so excited.

"I won't keep you here against your will," Toby told him.

His cell phone rang. He turned away to answer it and the kids eagerly moved to the railing to better see the carolers.

Toby tapped Marla's shoulder, then handed her the phone.

Marla took it and moved down the porch out of hearing with it, her expression one of great happiness.

Toby squatted down beside Cindy to get her attention. "There's someone on the phone that wants to say Merry Christmas. The call is coming from Eastern Europe."

Without a word, Cindy rushed to where Marla was chatting a mile a minute on the phone. Marla handed the phone to her sister who took over speaking excitedly to the caller.

Toby stepped to Victor who only then turned and noticed his sisters down the porch and as happy as he had ever seen them.

"Who's on the phone?" he asked.

"Your mom and dad."

Victor dashed to join his sisters and get his turn on the phone.

Febbraro smiled at Toby who said, "I'm sure I'll get my official Santa Claus helper badge for arranging that call. And their parents helped avoid a messy problem and will be properly rewarded because a certain someone wanted them out of the country so she could use their kids. They won't thank her but will appreciate the twist. And the man she squeezed to arrange things is out and maybe will want revenge."

Febbraro gives him a friendly punch on the arm, then put an arm around him and gave him a hug. "You did good all around, Toby."

* * *

A few minutes and two carols later, Dragenlyte and Noble stood at the living room window watching as the others all joined the carolers and moved off up the street.

Noble said, "I didn't expect to come right out with it that way but there it is. Honesty must be some side effect of the holiday spirit."

"I'm glad you said you like children but don't want any around all the time so I won't waste energy pretending to be all maternal."

"I have to admit to reservations about your goal in this case but I am impressed with your skill at calling in resources and getting the needed relevant information when you want something done."

"Since I'm now committed by my own words to being Ms. Nice Person for at least several months, I'll have to shift my goals and see how much more good I can do."

"You can start right now by agreeing to make me happy. That would be a good thing, wouldn't it?"

"I need particulars before I can say."

"Come caroling with me right now. Then come on a Caribbean cruise with me next weekend."

"In the spirit of generosity deeply tinged with self-interest, I'll agree to both."

"You wouldn't be the woman I'm so taken with any other way. I haven't always been a hundred and ten percent above board but I've kept myself at least under that much control. Lately I've been seeing more and more things going on that I feel I should help control for the good of the world. But that'd be more fun and successful with the help of someone with years of experience planning outside the box," he said.

* * *

When Noble and Dragenlyte ambled up to join them, the group of carolers included the Gordon children, Febbraro, Wurster, Quade, Klemper, Bob Lapinski and his mom.

They were singing outside Rudolf Rambler's house. His hang glider was on the lawn and he was at the door.

Toby stood back from everyone making a cell phone call.

Pawling answered, "I'm not here, I went to Moscow. I won't use a fake accent and try to confuse you about which one. This is a live recording."

"Shane, my good man, this is Toby. I wanted you to know that the Dragon Lady is out here with us at the moment so you can relax. She won't be coming after you. No need to hide or wear disguises."

"Does that mean you failed?"

"Oddly enough, I succeeded more than I could have expected. I'll give you the details some day soon."

"Let me be clear on this, she's not searching for me to punish me for helping you?"

"The situation has changed and she's forgotten all about that. She doesn't need to use the kids anymore, therefore she has a healthier relationship with everyone."

"Is that a CD you're playing?"

"No, it's live carolers repeating the classic scenes of Christmas Eve. Sorry you can't be here to see it."

"So you're adventure has a happy ending. What are you gonna call it when you write a book about it?"

"I think *Down the Chimney They Came* would pretty much wrap it up."

"I'm glad you called. I will relax at least some now."

"No, you can totally relax and enjoy the holidays."

"There's lots you don't know, which is probably just as well. Like that that was not the only scary thing I have going on today."

"See, we'll each have a story to tell. I'm eager to hear what I'm sure based on my experiences knowing you I won't be able to even think about topping. We'll get together soon."

"Yeah, I'm curious and I'm owed big time."

"Merry Christmas to all," Toby said.

"And to all a good night," Pawling said.